THE CROWD ROARED

Behind his shield, Tyl grinned—if that was the right word for the way instinct drew up the corners of his mouth to bare his teeth.

Something pinged on the railing. Tyl's gun quivered, pointed—

"Wait!" thundered the bull-horn.

"My people!" boomed President Delcorio's voice from the roofline. He rested his palms wide apart on the railing.

He'd followed after all, a step behind the Slammers officer just in case a sniper was waiting for the first motion.

The mob was making a great deal of disconnected noise. Delcorio trusted his amplified voice to carry him through as he continued, "I have dismissed the miscreant Berne as you demanded. I will turn him over to the custody of the Church for safekeeping until the entire State can determine the punishment for his many crimes."

"Give us Berne!" snarled the bull-horn with echoing violence. It spoke in the voice of a priest but not a Christian; and the mob that took up the chant was not even human.

DAVID DRAKE
HAMMER'S
COUNTING THE COST
Slammers

BAEN BOOKS

COUNTING THE COST

Copyright 1987 by David Drake

A Baen Books Original

Baen Publishing Enterprises
260 Fifth Avenue
New York, N.Y. 10001

First printing, November 1987

ISBN: 0-671-65355-5

Cover art by Paul Alexander

Printed in the United States of America

Distributed by
SIMON & SCHUSTER
1230 Avenue of the Americas
New York, N.Y. 10020

DEDICATION

To Sergeant Ronnie Hembree
Who did good work.

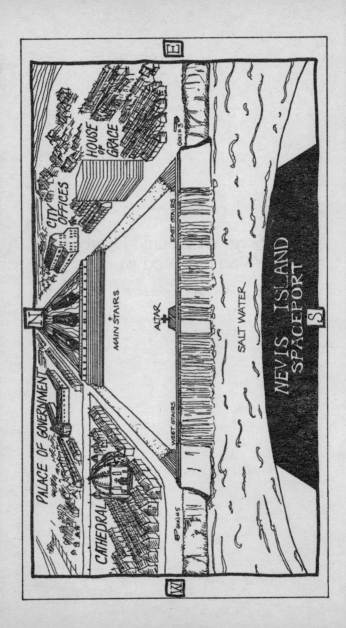

CHAPTER ONE

They'd told Tyl Koopman that Bamberg City's starport was on an island across the channel from the city proper, so he hadn't expected much of a skyline when the freighter's hatches opened.

Neither had he expected a curtain of steam boiling up so furiously that the sun was only a bright patch in mid-sky.

Tyl stepped back with a yelp. The crewman at the controls of the giant cargo doors laughed and said, "Well, you were in such a *hurry*, soldier. . . ."

The Slammers-issue pack Tyl carried was all the luggage he'd brought from six month's furlough on Miesel. Strapped to the bottom of the pack was a case of home-made jalapeño jelly that his aunt was sure—correctly—was better than any he could get elsewhere in the galaxy.

But altogether, the weight of Tyl's gear was much less than he was used to carrying in weap-

1

ons, rations, and armor when he led a company of Alois Hammer's infantry. He turned easily and looked at the crewman with mild sadness—the visage of a dog that's been unexpectedly kicked . . . and maybe just enough else beneath the sadness to be disquieting.

The crewman looked down at his controls, then again to the mercenary waiting to disembark. The squealing stopped when the triple hatches locked open. "Ah," called the crewman, "it'll clear up in a minute er two. It's always like this on Bamberg the first couple ships down after a high tide. The port floods, y'see, and it always looks like half the bloody ocean's waiting in the hollows t' burn off."

The steam—the hot mist; it'd never been dangerous, Tyl realized how—was thinning quickly. From the hatchway he could see the concrete pad and, in the near distance, the bulk of the freighter that must have landed just before theirs. The flecks beyond the concrete were the inevitable froth speckling moving water, the channel or the ocean itself—and the water looked cursed close to somebody who'd just spent six months on a place as dry as Miesel.

"Where do they put the warehouses?" Tyl asked. "Don't they flood?"

"Every three months or so they would," the crewman agreed. "That's why they're on the mainland, in Bamberg City, where there's ten meters of cliff and seawall t' keep 'em dry. But out here's flat, and I guess they figured they'd sooner the landing point be on the island in case somebody, you know, landed a mite hard."

The crewman grinned tightly. Tyl grinned back. They were both professionals in fields that involved risks. People who couldn't joke about the risks of the jobs they'd chosen tended to find other lines of work in a hurry.

The ones who survived.

"Well, I guess it's clear," Tyl said with enough question in his tone to expect a warning if he were wrong. "There'll be ground transport coming?"

"Yeah, hovercraft from Bamberg real soon," the crewman agreed. "But look, there's a shelter on the other side a' that bucket there. You might want to get over to it right quick. There's some others in orbit after us, and it can be pretty interesting t' be out on the field when it's this wet and there's more ships landing."

Tyl nodded to the man and strode down the ramp that had been the lower third of the hatch door. He was nervous, but it'd all be fine soon. He'd be back with his unit and not alone, the way he'd been on the ship—

And for the whole six months he'd spent with his family and a planet full of civilians who understood his words but not his language.

The mainland shore, a kilometer across Nevis Channel, was a corniche. The harsh cliffs were notched by the mouth of the wide river which was responsible for Bamberg City's location and the fact it was the only real city on the planet. Tyl hadn't gotten the normal briefing because the regiment shifted employers while he was on furlough, but the civilian sources available on Miesel when he got his movement orders were about all he needed anyway.

Captain Tyl Koopman wasn't coming to the planet Bamberia; he was returning to Hammer's Slammers. After five years in the regiment and six months back with his family, he had to agree with the veterans who'd warned him before he went on furlough that he wasn't going home.

He had left home, because the Slammers were the only home he'd got.

The shelter was a low archway, translucent green from the outside and so unobtrusive that Tyl might have overlooked it if there had been any other structure on the island. He circled to one end, apprehensive of the rumbling he heard in the sky—and more than a little nervous about the pair of star freighters already grounded in the port.

The ships were quiescent. They steamed and gave off pings of differential cooling, but for the next few days they weren't going to move any more than would buildings of the same size. Nevertheless, learned reflex told Tyl that big metal objects were tanks . . . and no infantryman lived very long around tanks without developing a healthy respect for them.

The door opened automatically as Tyl reached for it, wondering where the latch was. Dim shadows swirled inside the shelter, behind a second panel that rotated aside only when the outside door had closed again.

There were a dozen figures spaced within a shelter that had room for hundreds. All those waiting were human; all were male; and all but one were in civilian garb.

Tyl walked toward the man in uniform—almost toward him, while almost meeting the other man's eyes so that he could stop and find a clear spot at the long window if the fellow glared or turned his head as the Slammers officer approached.

No problem, though. The fellow's quirking grin suggested that he was as glad of the company as Tyl was.

It was real easy to embarrass yourself when you didn't know the rules—and when nobody wore the rank tabs that helped you figure out what those rules might be.

From within the shelter, the windows had an extreme clarity that proved they were nothing as simple as glass or thermoplastic. The shelter was unfurnished, without even benches, but its construction proved that Bamberia was a wealthy, high technology world.

There was a chance for real profit on this one. Colonel Hammer must have been delighted.

"Hammer's Regiment?" the waiting soldier asked, spreading his grin into a look of welcome.

"Captain Tyl Koopman," Tyl agreed, shaking the other man's hand. "I'd just gotten E Company when I went on furlough. But I don't know what may've happened since, you know, since we've shifted contracts."

He'd just blurted the thing that'd been bothering him ever since Command Central had sent the new location for him to report off furlough. He'd sweated blood to get that company command—sweated blood and spilled it . . . and the revised transit orders made him fear that he'd have to earn it all over again because he'd been gone on furlough when the Colonel needed somebody in the slot.

Tyl hadn't bothered to discuss it with the folks who'd been his friends and relatives when he was a civilian; they already looked at him funny from the time one of them asked about the scrimshaw he'd given her and he was drunk enough to tell the real story of the house-to-house on Cachalot. But this guy would understand, even though Tyl didn't know him and didn't even recognize the uniform.

"Charles Desoix," the man said, "United Defense Batteries." He flicked a collar tab with his finger. "Lieutenant and XO of Battery D, if you don't care what you say. It amounts to gopher, mainly. I just broke our Number Five gun out of Customs on Merrinet."

"Right, air defense," Tyl said with the enthusiasm of being able to place the man in a structured universe. "Calliopes?"

"Yeah," agreed Desoix with another broad grin, "and the inspectors seemed to think somebody in the crew had stuffed all eight barrels with drugs they were going to sell at our transfer stop on Merrinet. Might just've been right, too—but we needed the gun here more than they needed the evidence."

The ship that had been a rumble in the sky when Tyl ducked into the shelter was now within ten meters of the pad. The shelter's windows did an amazing job of damping vibration, but the concrete itself resonated like a drum to the freighter's engine note. The two soldiers fell silent. Tyl shifted his pack and studied Desoix.

The UDB uniform was black with silver piping that muted to non-reflective gray in service conditions. It was a little fancier than the Slammers' khaki—but Desoix's unit wasn't parade-ground pansies.

The Slammers provided their own defense against hostile artillery. Most outfits didn't have the luxury that Fire Central and the vehicle-mounted powerguns gave Hammer. Specialists like United Defense Batteries provided multi-barreled weapons —calliopes—to sweep the sky clear over defended positions and to accompany attacking columns which would otherwise be wrecked by shellfire.

It wasn't a job Tyl Koopman could imagine himself being comfortable doing; but Via! he didn't see himself leading a tank company either. A one-man skimmer and a 2 cm powergun were about all the hardware Tyl wanted to handle. Anything bigger cost him too much thought that would have been better spent on the human portion of his command.

"Your first time here?" Desoix asked diffidently. The third freighter was down. Though steam hissed away from the vessel with a high-pitched roar, it was possible to talk again.

Tyl nodded. Either the tide was falling rapidly or the first two ships had pretty well dried the pad for later comers. The billows of white mist were sparse enough that he could still see the city across the channel: or at any rate, he could see a twenty-story tower of metal highlights and transparent walls on one side of the river, and a domed structure across from it that gleamed gold—except for the ornate cross on the pinnacle whose core was living ruby.

"Not a bad place," Desoix said judiciously. He looked a few years older than the Slammers officer, but perhaps it was just that, looks, dark hair and thin features contrasting with Tyl's broad pale face and hair so blond that you could hardly see it when it was cropped as short as it was now.

"The city, I mean," Desoix said, modifying his earlier comment. "The sticks over on Continent Two where it looks like the fighting's going to be, well—they're the sticks."

He met Tyl's eyes. "I won't apologize for getting a quiet billet this time 'round."

"No need to," Tyl said . . . and they were both lying, because nobody who knows the difference brags to a combat soldier about a cushy assignment; and no combat soldier but wishes, somewhere in his heart of hearts, that *he'd* gotten the absolutely necessary assignment of protecting the capital while somebody else led troops into sniper-filled woodlands and endured the fluorescent drumbeat of hostile artillery.

But Via! *Somebody* had to do the job.

Both of them.

"Hey, maybe the next time," Tyl said with a false smile and a playful tap on the shoulder of the man who wasn't a stranger any more.

Several boats—hovercraft too small to haul more than a dozen men and their luggage—were putting out from Bamberg City, spraying their way toward the island with an enthusiasm that suggested they were racing.

Tyl's view of them was unexpectedly cut off when a huge surface-effect freighter slid in front of the shelter and settled. The freighter looked like a normal sub-sonic aircraft, but its airfoils were canted to double their lift by skimming over water or smooth ground. The bird couldn't really fly, but it could carry a thousand tonnes of cargo at 200 kph—a useful trade-off between true ships and true aircraft.

"Traders from Two," Desoix explained as men began scuttling from the freighter before its hydraulic outriggers had time to lock it firmly onto the pad. "They circle at a safe distance from the island while the starships are landing. Then, if they're lucky, they beat the Bamberg factors to the pad with the first shot at a deal."

He shrugged. "And if their luck's *really* out,

there's another starship on its way in about the time they tie up. Doesn't take much of a shock wave to make things real interesting aboard one of those."

Tyl squinted at the men scuttling from the surface-effect vehicle. Several of those waiting in the shelter were joining them, babbling and waving documents. "Say, those guys 're—"

"Yeah, rag-heads," Desoix agreed. "I mean, I'm sure they're in church every day, kissing crosses and all the proper things, but . . . yeah, they're looking at some problems if President Delcorio gets his crusade going."

"Well, that's what we're here for," Tyl said, looking around horizons that were hemmed by starships to the back and side and the surface-effect vehicle before him.

"Now," he added, controlling his grimace, "how do we get to the mainland if we're not cargo?"

"Ah, but we are," Desoix noted as he raised the briefcase that seemed to be all the luggage he carried. "Just not very valuable cargo, my friend. But I think it's about time to—"

As he started toward the door, one of the hovercars they'd watched put out from the city drove through the mingled cluster of men from the starships and the surface freighter. Water from the channel surrounded the car in a fine mist that cleared its path better than the threat of its rubber skirts. While the driver in his open cab exchanged curses with men from the surface freighter, the rear of his vehicle opened to disgorge half a dozen civilians in bright garments.

"Our transportation," Desoix said, nodding to the hovercar as he headed out of the shelter. "Now that it's dropped off the Bamberg factors to fight for their piece of the market. Everybody's got tobacco, and everybody wants a share of what may be the last cargoes onto the planet for a while."

"Before the shooting starts," Tyl amplified as he strode along with the UDB officer. They hadn't sent a briefing cube to Miesel for him . . . but it didn't take that or genius to figure out what was going to happen shortly after a world started hiring mercenary regiments.

"That's the betting," Desoix agreed. He opened the back of the car with his universal credit key, a computer chip encased in noble metal and banded to his wrist.

"Oh," said Tyl, staring at the keyed door.

"Yeah, everything's up to date here in Bamberg," said the other officer, stepping out of the doorway and waving Tyl through. "Hey!" he called to the driver. "My friend here's on me!"

"I can—" Tyl said.

"—delay us another ten minutes," Desoix broke in, "trying to charge this one to the Hammer account or pass the driver scrip from Lord knows where."

He keyed the door a second time and swung into the car, both men moving with the trained grace of soldiers who knew how to get on and off air cushion vehicles smoothly—because getting hung up was a good way to catch a round.

"Goes to the UDB account anyway," Desoix added. "Via, maybe we'll need a favor from you one of these days."

"I'm just not set up for this place, coming off furlough," Tyl explained. "It's not like, you know, Colonel Hammer isn't on top of things."

The driver fluffed his fans and the car began to cruise in cautious arcs around the starships, looking for other passengers. All the men they saw were busy with merchants or with the vessels themselves, preparing the rails and gantries that would load the vacuum-sealed one-tonne bales of Bamberg tobacco when the factors had struck their deals.

No one looked at the car with more than idle interest. The driver spun his vehicle back into the channel with a lurch and building acceleration.

CHAPTER TWO

"One thing," Desoix said, looking out the window even though the initial spray cloaked the view. "Money's no problem here. Any banking booth can access Hammer's account and probably your account back home if it's got a respondent on one of the big worlds. Perfectly up to date. But, ah, don't talk to anybody here about religion, all right?"

He met Tyl's calm eyes. "No matter how well you know them, you don't know them that well. Here. And don't go out except wearing your uniform. They don't bother soldiers, especially mercs; but somebody might make a mistake if you were in civilian clothes."

Their vehicle was headed for the notch in the sea cliffs. It was a river mouth as Tyl had assumed from the spaceport, but human engineering had overwhelmed everything natural about the site.

13

The river was covered and framed into a triangular plaza by concrete seawalls as high as those reinforcing the corniche.

Salt water from the tide-choked sea even now gleamed on the plaza, just as it was streaming from the spaceport. Figures—women as well as men, Tyl thought, though it was hard to be sure between the spray and the loose costumes they wore here—were pouring into the plaza as fast as the water had left it.

For the most part the walls were sheer and ten meters high, but there were broad stairs at each apex of the plaza—two along the seaside east and west and a third, defended by massive flood works, that must have been built over the channel of the river itself.

"What's the problem?" Tyl asked calmly. From what he'd read, the battle lines on Bamberia were pretty clearly drawn. The planetary government was centered on Continent One—wealthy and very centralized, because the Pink River drained most of the arable land on the continent. All the uniquely-flavorful Bamberg tobacco could be barged at minimal cost to Bamberg City and loaded in bulk onto starships.

There hadn't been much official interest in Continent Two for over a century after the main settlement. There was good land on Two, but it was patchy and not nearly as easy to develop profitably as One proved.

That didn't deter other groups who saw a chance that looked good by their standards. Small starships touched down in little market centers. Everything was on a lesser scale; prices, quantities, and profit margins. . . .

But in time, the estimated total grew large

enough for the central government to get interested. Official trading ports were set up on the coast of Two. Local tobacco was to be sent from them to Bamberg City, to be assessed and transshipped.

Some was; but the interloping traders continued to land in the back country, and central government officials gnashed their teeth over tax revenues that were all the larger for being illusory.

It didn't help that One had been settled by Catholic Fundamentalists from Germany and Latin America, and that the squatters on Two were almost entirely Levantine Muslims.

The traders didn't care. They had done their business in holographic entertainment centers and solar-powered freezers, but there was just as much profit in powerguns and grenades.

As for mercenaries like Alois Hammer—and Tyl Koopman. . . They couldn't be said not to care; because if there wasn't trouble, they didn't have work.

Not that Tyl figured there was much risk of galactic peace being declared.

Desoix laughed without even attempting to make the sound humorous. "Well," he said, "do you know when Easter is?"

"Huh?" said Tyl. "My family wasn't, you know, real religious . . . and anyway, do you mean on Earth or here or where?"

"That's the question, isn't it?" Desoix answered, glancing around the empty cabin just to be *sure* there couldn't be a local listening to him.

"Some folks here," he continued, "figure Easter according to Earth-standard days. You can tell them because they've always got something red in their clothing, a cap or a ribbon around their sleeve if nothing else. And the folks that say, 'We're on Bamberia so God meant us to use Bamberg days to figure his calendar . . . ,' well, they wear black.

"And the people who wear cloaks, black *or* red," Desoix concluded. "Make sure they know you're a soldier. Because they'd just as soon knock your head in as that of any policeman or citizen—but they won't, because they know that killing soldiers gets expensive fast."

Tyl shook his head. "I'd say I didn't believe it," he said with the comfortable superiority of somebody commenting on foolishness to which he doesn't subscribe. "But sure, it's no screwier than a lot of places. People don't need a reason to have problems, they make their own."

"And they hire us," agreed Desoix.

"Well, they hire us to give 'em more control over the markets on Two," Tyl said, not quite arguing. "This time around."

Their vehicle was approaching the plaza. It stood two meters above the channel, barely eye-height to the men in the back of the hovercar. A pontoon-mounted landing stage slid with the tides in a vertical slot in the center of the dam blocking the river beneath the plaza; the car slowed as they approached the stage.

"If they dam the river—" Tyl started to say, because he wouldn't have commanded a company of the Slammers had he not assessed the terrain about him as a matter of course.

Before Desoix could answer, slotted spillways opened at either end of the dam and whipped the channel into froth with gouts of fresh water under enough pressure to fling it twenty meters from the concrete. The hovercar, settling as it made its final approach to the stage, bobbed in the ripples; the driver must have been cursing the operator who started to drain the impoundment now instead of a minute later.

"Hydraulics they know about," Desoix commented as their vehicle grounded on the stage with a blip of its fans and the pontoons rocked beneath them. "They can't move the city—it's here because of the river, floods or no. But for twenty kilometers upstream, they've built concrete levees. When the tides peak every three months or so—as they just did—they close the gates here and divert the river around Bamberg City."

He pointed up the coast. "When the tide goes down a little, they vent water through the main channel again until everything's normal. In about two days, they can let barges across to the spaceport."

The hovercar's door opened, filling the back with the roar of the water jetting from a quarter kilometer to either side. "Welcome to Bamberg City," Desoix shouted over the background as he motioned Tyl ahead of him.

The Slammers officer paused outside the vehicle to slip on his pack again. Steel-mesh stairs extended through the landing stage, up to the plaza—but down into the water as well: they did not move with the stage or the tides, and they were dripping and as slick as wet, polished metal could be.

"No gear?" he asked his companion curiously.

Desoix waved his briefcase. "Some, but I'm leaving it to be off-loaded with the gun. Remember, I'm travelling with a whole curst calliope."

"Well, you must be glad to have it back," said

Tyl as he gripped the slick railing before he attempted the steps.

"Not as glad as my battery commander, Major Borodin," Desoix said with a chuckle. "It was his ass, not mine, if the Merrinet authorities had decided to keep it till it grew whiskers."

"But—" he added over the clang of his boots and Tyl's as they mounted the stairs, "—he's not a bad old bird, the Major, and he cuts me slack that not every CO might be willing to do."

The stairs ended on a meter-wide walkway that was part of the plaza but separated from it by a low concrete building, five meters on the side parallel to the dam beneath it—and narrower in the other dimension. On top, facing inward to the plaza, was an ornate, larger than life, crucifix.

Tyl hesitated, uncertain as to which way to walk around the building. He'd expected somebody from his unit to be waiting here on the mainland if not at the spaceport itself. He was feeling alone again. The raucous babble of locals setting up sales kiosks on the plaza increased his sense of isolation.

"Either way," Desoix said, putting a hand on the other man's shoulder—in comradeship as well as direction. "This is just the mechanical room for the locks—except—"

Desoix leaned over so that his lips were almost touching Tyl's ear and said, "Except that it's the altar of Christ the Redeemer, if you ask anybody here. I *really* put my foot in it when I tried to get permission to site one of my guns on it. Would've been a perfect place to cover the sea approaches, but it seems that they'd rather die here than have their cross moved.

"Of course," the UDB officer added, a professional who didn't want another professional to think that he'd done a bad job of placing his guns, "I found an all-right spot on a demolition site just east of here."

Desoix nodded toward the thronged steps at the eastern end of the plaza. "Not quite the arc of fire, but nothing we can't cover from the other guns. Especially now we've got Number Five back."

In the time it had taken the hovercar to navigate from the spaceport to the mainland, a city of small shops had sprung up in the plaza. Tyl couldn't imagine the development could be orderly—but it was, at least to the extent that a field of clover has order, because the individual plants respond to general stimuli that force them into patterns.

There were city police present, obvious from their peaked caps, green uniforms, and needle stunners worn on white cross-belts . . . but they were not organizing the ranks of kiosks. Men and women in capes were doing that; and after a glance at their faces, Tyl didn't need Desoix to tell him how tough they thought they were.

They just might be right, too; but things have a way of getting a lot worse than anybody expected, and it was then that you got a good look at what you and the rest of your crew were really made of.

Traffic in the plaza was entirely pedestrian. Vehicles were blocked from attempting the staircases at either sea-front corner by massive steel bollards, and the stairs at the remaining apex were closed by what seemed to be lockworks as massive as those venting the river beneath the plaza. They'd *have* to be, Tyl realized, because there needed to be some way of releasing water from the top of its levee-channelled course in event of an emergency.

But that wasn't a problem for Captain Tyl Koopman just now. What *he* needed was somebody wearing the uniform of Hammer's Slammers, and he sure as blazes didn't see such in all this throng.

"Ah," he said, "Lieutenant . . . do you—"

The transceiver implanted in his mastoid bone beeped, and an unfamiliar voice began to answer Tyl's question before he had fully formed it.

"Transit Base to Captain Tyl Koopman," said the implant, scratchy with static and the frustration of the man at the other end of the radio link. "Captain Koopman, are you reading me? Over."

Tyl felt a rush of relief as he willed his left little finger to crook. The finger didn't move, but the redirected nerve impulse triggered the transmitter half of his implant. "Koopman to Transit," he said harshly. "Where in *blazes* are you, anyway? Over."

"Sir," said the voice, "this is Sergeant Major Scratchard, and you don't need to hear that I'm sorry about the cock-up. There's an unscheduled procession, and I can't get into the main stairs until it's over. If you'll tell me where you are, I swear I'll get t' you as soon as the little boys put away their crosses and let the men get back to work."

"I'm—" Tyl began. Desoix was turned half aside to indicate that he knew of the conversation going on and knew it wasn't any of this business. That gave the Slammers officer the mental base he needed for a reasoned decision rather than nervously agreeing to wait in place.

"Ah, sir," Scratchard continued; he'd paused but not broken the transmission. "There's a load of stuff for you here from Central. The Colonel wants you to lead the draft over when you report to Two. And, ah, the President, ah, Delcorio, wants to see you ASAP because you're the ranking officer now. Over."

"The main stairs," Tyl said, aloud rather than sub-vocalizing the way he had done thus far through the implant. Desoix could hear him. To underscore that he *wanted* the UDB officer to listen, Tyl pointed toward the empty stairs at the third apex. "That's at the end farthest from the sea, then?"

Desoix nodded. Scratchard's voice said, "Ah, yessir," through the static.

"Fine, I'll meet you there when you can get through," Tyl said flatly. "I'm in uniform and I have one pack is all. Koopman over and out."

He smiled to Desoix. "It'll give me a chance to look around," he explained. Now that his unit had contacted him he felt confident—whole, for the first time in . . . Via, in six months, just about.

Desoix smiled back. "Well, you shouldn't have any real problems here," he said. "But—" his head tilted, just noticeably, in the direction of three red-cloaked toughs "don't forget what I told you. Myself, I'm going to check Number Three gun so long as I'm down on the corniche anyway. See you around, soldier."

"See you around," Tyl agreed confidently. He grinned at his surroundings with a tourist's vague interest. Captain Tyl Koopman was home again, or he would be in a few minutes.

CHAPTER THREE

Charles Desoix thought about the House of Grace as he mounted the eastern stairs from the plaza. The huge hospital building, Bishop Trimer's latest but not necessarily last attempt to impose his presence on Bamberg City, was about all a man could see as he left the plaza in this direction. For that matter, the twenty glittering stories of the House of Grace were the only portions of the city visible from the floor of the plaza, over the sea walls.

It was like looking at a block of blue ice; and it was the only thing about being stationed in Bamberg City that Desoix could really have done without. But the Bishop certainly wasn't enough of a problem that Desoix intended to transfer to one of the batteries out in the boonies on Two, rumbling through valleys you could be *sure* the rag-heads had mined and staked for snipers.

Thousands of people, shoppers as well as shop-

keepers, were still pouring into the plaza; Desoix
was almost alone in wanting to go in the opposite
direction. He wasn't in a big hurry, so he kept his
temper in check. An unscheduled inspection of
Gun Three was a good excuse for the battery XO
to be there, not just sneaking around. . . .

He had some business back at the Palace of
Government, too; but he wasn't so horny from the
trip to Merrinet that he was willing to make that
his *first* priority. Quite.

Three prostitutes, each of them carried by a
pair of servants to save their sandals and gossamer
tights, were on their way to cribs in the plaza
below. Desoix made way with a courteous bow;
but uniform or not, he was going to make way.
The phalanx of red-cloaked guards surrounding
the girls would have made sure of that.

One of the girls smiled at Desoix as she rocked
past. He smiled back at her, thinking of Anne
McGill . . . but Blood and *Martyrs!* he could last
another half hour. He'd get his job done first.

There was an unusual amount of congestion here,
but that was because the main stairs were blocked.
Another procession, no doubt; Bishop Trimer
playing his games while President Delcorio and
his wife tried to distract the populace with a crusade on Two.

As for the populace, its members knocked in
each other's heads depending on what each was
wearing that day.

Just normal politics, was all. Normal for places
that hired the United Defense Batteries and other
mercenary regiments, at any rate.

At dawn, the shadow of the House of Grace lay
across the Cathedral on the other side of the plaza,
so that the gilded dome no longer gleamed. Desoix

wrinkled his nose and thought about dust-choked roads on Two with a sniper every hundred meters of the wooded ridges overlooking them.

To blazes with all of them.

There was even more of a crush at the head of the stairs. Vehicles slid up to the bollards to drop their cargo and passengers—and then found themselves blocked by later-comers, furious at being stopped a distance from where they wanted to be. A squad of city police made desultory efforts to clear the jam, but they leaped aside faster than the bystanders did when the real fighting started.

Two drivers, one with a load of produce and the other carrying handbags, were snarling. Three black-cloaked toughs jumped the driver with the red headband, knocked him down, and linked arms in a circle about the victim so that they could all three put the boot in.

At least a dozen thugs in red coalesced from nowhere around the fight. It grew like a crystal in a supersaturated solution of hate.

The police had their stunners out and were radioing for help, but they kept their distance. The toughs wore body armor beneath their cloaks, and Desoix heard the slam of at least one slug-throwing pistol from the ruck.

He willed his body to stay upright and to stride with swift dignity between vehicles and out of the potential line of fire. It would have griped his soul to run from this scum; but more important, anyone who ducked and scurried was a worthy victim, while a recognized mercenary was safe except by accident.

Anyway, that was what Desoix told himself.

But by the Lord! it felt good to get out of the shouted violence and see Gun Three, its six-man

crew alert and watching the trouble at the stairhead with their personal weapons ready.

The calliope's eight stubby barrels were mounted
on the back of a large air-cushion truck. Instead of
rotating through a single loading station as did the
2 cm tri-barrels on the Slammers' combat cars,
each of the calliope's tubes was a separate gun.
The array gimballed together to fire on individual
targets which the defenders couldn't afford to miss.

Any aircraft, missile, or artillery shell that came
over the sector of the horizon which Gun Three
scanned—when the weapon was live—would be
met by a pulse of high-intensity 3 cm bolts from
the calliope's eight barrels. Nothing light enough
to fly through the air could survive that raking.

A skillful enemy could saturate the gun's defensive screen by launching simultaneous attacks from
several directions, but even then the interlocking
fire of a full, properly-sited six-calliope battery
should be able to hold out and keep the target it
defended safe.

Of course, proper siting was an ideal rather
than a reality, since every irregularity of terrain—or
a building like the House of Grace—kept guns
from supporting one another as they could do on a
perfectly flat surface. Bamberg City wasn't likely
to be surrounded by hostile artillery batteries,
though, and Charles Desoix was proud of the single-
layer coverage he had arranged for the whole pop-
ulated area.

He did hope his gunners had sense enough not
to talk about saturating coverage when they were
around civilians. Especially civilians who looked
like they'd been born to squatter families on Two.

"Good to see you back, sir," said Blaney, the
sergeant in command of Gun Three on this watch.

He was a plump man and soft looking, but he'd reacted well in an emergency on Hager's World, taking manual control of his calliope and using it in direct fire on a party of sappers that had made it through the perimeter Federal forces were trying to hold.

"Say," asked a blond private Desoix couldn't call by name until his eye caught stenciling on the fellow's helmet: Karsov. "Is there any chance we're going to move, sir? Farther away from all this? It gets worse every day."

"What's . . . " Desoix began with a frown, but he turned to view the riot again before he finished the question—and then he didn't have to finish it.

The riot that Desoix had put out of his mind by steely control had expanded like mold on bread while he walked the three hundred meters to the shelter of his gun and its crew. There must have been nearly a thousand people involved—many of them lay-folk with the misfortune of being caught in the middle, but at least half were the cloaked shock troops of the two Easter factions.

Knives and metal bars flashed in the air. A shotgun thumped five times rapidly into a chorus of screams.

"Via," Desoix muttered.

A firebomb went off, spraying white trails of burning magnesium through the curtain of petroleum flames. Police air cars were hovering above the crowd on the thrust of their ducted fans while uniformed men hosed the brawlers indiscriminately with their needle stunners.

"This is what we're defending?" Blaney asked with heavy irony.

Desoix squatted, motioning the gun crew down with him. No point in having a stray round hit somebody. The men were wearing their body armor, but Desoix himself wasn't. He didn't need it on shipboard or during negotiations on Merrinet, and it hadn't struck him how badly the situation in Bamberg City could deteriorate in the two weeks he was gone.

"Well," he said, more or less in answer. "They're the people paying us until we hear different. Internal politics, that's not our business. And anyhow, it looks like the police have it pretty well under control."

"For now," muttered Karsov.

The fighting had melted away, as much in reaction to the firebomb as to the efforts of the civil authorities. Thugs were carrying away injured members of their own parties. The police tossed the disabled battlers whom they picked up into air cars with angry callousness.

"It'd be kinda nice, sir," said Blaney, turning his eyes toward the House of Grace towering above them, "if we could maybe set up on top of there. Get a nice view all around, you know, good for defense; and, ah, we wouldn't need worry about getting hit with the odd brick or the like if the trouble comes this way next time."

The chorus of assent from the whole crew indicated that they'd been discussing the point at length among themselves.

Desoix smiled. He couldn't blame the men, but wishing something strongly didn't make it a practical solution.

"Look," he said, letting his eyes climb the sculptured flank of the hospital building as he spoke. The narrower sides of the House of Grace, the north and south faces, were of carven stone rather than chrome and transparent panels.

The south face, toward Gun Three and the sea
front, was decorated with the miracles of Christ:
the sick rising from their beds; the lame tossing
away their crutches; loaves and fishes multiplying
miraculously to feed the throng stretching back in
low relief.

On the opposite side were works of human
mercy: the poor being fed and lodged in church
kitchens; orphans being raised to adulthood; med-
ical personnel with crosses on their uniforms healing the sick as surely as Christ did on the south
face.

But over the works of human mercy, the ascetic
visage of Bishop Trimer presided in a coruscance
of sun-rays like that which haloed Christ on the
opposite face. A determined man, Bishop Trimer.
And very sure of himself.

"Look," Desoix repeated as he reined in his
wandering mind. "In the first place, it's a bad
location because the gun can only depress three
degrees and that'd leave us open to missiles skimming the surface."

Karsov opened his mouth as if to argue, but a
snarled order from Sergeant Blaney shut him up.
Lieutenant Desoix was easy-going under normal
circumstances; but he was an officer and the Battery XO . . . and he was also hard as nails when
he chose to be, as Blaney knew by longer experience than the private had.

"But more important . . ." Desoix went on
with a nod of approval to Blaney. "Never site a
gun in a spot where you can't drive away if things
really get bad. Do you expect to ride down in the
elevators if a mob decides what they really ought
to do tomorrow is burn the hospital?"

"Well, they wouldn't . . ." Karsov began.

He looked at the wreckage and smoke near the plaza stairs and thought the better of saying what a mob would or wouldn't do.

"Were you on Shinano, Sergeant?" Desoix asked Blaney.

"Yessir," the non-com said. "But I wasn't in the city during the riots, if that's what you mean."

"I was a gun captain then," Desoix said with a smile and a lilting voice, because it was always nice to remember the ones you survived. "The Battery Commander—this was Gilt, and they sacked him for it—sited us on top of the Admin Building. Ten stories in a central park.

"So we had a *really* good view of the mob, because parts of it were coming down all five radial streets with torches. And they'd blown up the transformer station providing power to the whole center of town.

He coughed and rubbed his face. "There were air cars flying every which way, carrying business-men who knew they weren't going to get out at ground level . . . but we didn't have a car, and we couldn't even get the blazes off the roof. It didn't have a staircase, just the elevator—and that quit when the power went off."

Blaney was nodding with grim agreement; so were two of the other veterans in the gun crew.

"How—how'd you get out, sir?" Karsov asked in a suitably chastened tone.

Desoix grinned again. It wasn't a pleasant ex-pression. "Called to one of those businessmen on a loud-hailer," he said. "Asked him to come pick us up. When he saw where we had the calliope pointed, he decided that was a good idea."

The slim officer paused and looked up at the House of Grace again. "Getting lucky once doesn't mean I'm going to put any of my men in that particular bucket again, though," he said. "Down here—" he smiled brightly, but there was more than pure humor in this expression too "—at the worst, you've got the gun to keep anybody at a distance."

"Think it's going to be that bad, sir?" one of the crewmen asked.

Desoix shrugged. "I need to report to the Palace," he said. "I guess it's clear enough to do that now."

As he turned to walk away from the gun position, he heard Sergeant Blaney saying, "Not for us and the other mercs, maybe. But yeah, it's going to get that bad here. You wait and see."

CHAPTER FOUR

Tyl Koopman strolled through a series of the short aisles into which the plaza was marked by freshly-erected kiosks. In most cases the shop proprietors were still setting out their goods, but they were willing to call Tyl over to look at their merchandise. He smiled and walked on—the smile becoming fixed in short order.

He'd learned Spanish when the Slammers were stationed on Cartagena three years before, so he could have followed the local language without difficulty. It was interesting that most of the shopkeepers recognized Tyl's uniform and spoke to him in Dutch, fluent at least for a few words of enticement.

It was interesting also that many of those keeping shops in the plaza were of Levantine extraction, like the merchants who had disembarked from the surface-effect freighter. They were no-

33

ticeable not only for their darker complexions but also because their booths and clothing were so bedecked with crosses that sometimes the color of the underlying fabric was doubtful.

Not, as Lieutenant Desoix had suggested, that their desperate attempts to belong to the majority would matter a hoot in Hell when the Crusade really got moving. Tyl wasn't a cynic. Like most line mercenaries, he wasn't enough of an intellectual to have abstract positions about men and politics.

But he had a good mind and plenty of data about the way things went when politicians hired men to kill for them.

The section Tyl was walking through was given over to tobacco and smoking products—shops for visitors rather than staples for the domestic market which seemed to fill most of the plaza.

Tobacco from Bamberia had a smooth melding of flavors that remained after the raw leaf was processed into the cold inhalers in which most of the galaxy used imported tobacco. Those who couldn't afford imports smoked what they grew in local plots on a thousand worlds . . . but those who could afford the best and wanted the creosote removed before they put the remainder of the taste into their bodies, bought from Bamberia.

Most of the processing was done off-planet, frequently on the user world where additional flavorings were added to the inhalers to meet local tastes. There were a few inhaler factories on the outskirts of Bamberg City, almost the only manufacturing in a metropolis whose wealth was based on transport and government. Their creations were displayed on the tables in the plaza, brightly-colored plastic tubes whose shapes counterfeited everything from cigarillos to cigars big enough to pass for riot batons.

But the local populace tended to follow traditional methods of using the herb that made them rich. Products for the local market posed here as exotica for the tourists and spacers who wanted something to show the folks back home where they'd been.

Tourists and spacers and mercenaries. The number of kiosks serving outsiders must have increased radically since President Delcorio started hiring mercenaries for his Crusade.

Tyl passed by displays of smoking tobacco and hand-rolled cigars—some of the boxes worth a week's pay to him, even now that he had his captaincy. There were cigar cutters and pipe cleaners, cigarette holders and pipes carved from microporous meerschaum mined on the coasts of Two.

Almost all the decoration was religious: crosses, crucifixes, and other symbols of luxuriant Christianity. That theme was almost as noticeable to Tyl as the fact that almost everyone in the plaza—and every kiosk—was decorated with either black or red, and never both.

Each staggering aisle was of uniform background. To underscore the situation, cloaked toughs faced off at every angle where the two colors met, glowering threats that did not quite—while Tyl saw them—come to open violence.

Great place to live, Bamberg City. Tyl was glad of his khaki uniform. He wondered how often the silver and black of the United Defense Batteries was mistaken for black by somebody with a red cloak and a brick in his hand.

Grimacing to himself, the Slammers officer strode more swiftly toward his goal, the empty stairs at the north end of the plaza. The scene around him was colorful, all right, and this was probably one of the few chances he'd have to see it.

You served on a lot of worlds in a mercenary regiment, but what you mostly *saw* there were other soldiers and the wrack of war . . . which was universal, a smoky gray ambiance that you scanned and maybe shot at before you moved on.

Even so, Tyl didn't want to spend any longer than he had to in this plaza. He could feel the edge of conflict which overlay it like the cloaks that covered the weapons and armor of the omnipresent bullies, waiting for an opportunity to strike out. He'd seen plenty of fighting during his years with the Slammers, but he didn't want it hovering around him when he was supposed to be in a peaceful rear area.

The stairs were slimy with water pooling in low spots, but Nevis Island and its spaceport shielded the plaza from most of the sea-weed and marine life that the high tides would otherwise have washed up. Tyl picked his way carefully, since he seemed to be the first person to climb them since the tide dropped.

A procession, Scratchard had said, blocking normal traffic. Maybe that would be a little easier to take than the human bomb waiting to go off below in the plaza.

At the top of the stairs were ten pairs of steel-and-concrete doors. Each side-hung panel was five meters across and at least three meters high. The doors—lock-gates—were fully open now. They rotated out toward the plaza on trunnions in slotted rails set into the concrete. As Tyl neared them on his lonely climb, he heard the sound of chanted music echoing from beyond the doors.

Tyl had expected to see gaily-bedecked vehicles when he reached the top of the stairs and could look into the covered mall beyond. Instead there were people on foot, and most of *them* were standing rather than marching from left to right.

The mall was at least a hundred meters wide; its pavement was marked to pass heavy ground traffic from one side of the river to the other. At the moment, a sparse line of priests in full regalia was walking slowly down the center of the expanse, interspersed with lay-folk wearing robes of ceremonially-drab coarseness.

Some carried objects on display. Ornate crucifixes were the most common, but there were banners and a reliquary borne by four women which, if *pure* gold, must have cost as much as a starship.

Every few paces, the marchers paused and chanted something in Latin. When they began to move again, a refrain boomed back from the line of solid-looking men in white robes on either side of the procession route. The guards—they could be nothing else—wore gold crosses on the left shoulders of their garments, but they also bore meter-long staffs.

There was no need for the procession to be blocking the whole width of the mall; but when Tyl stepped through the door, the nearest men in white gave him a look that made it real clear what would happen to anybody who tried to carry out secular business in an area the Church had marked for its own.

Tyl stopped. He stood in a formal posture in-

stead of lounging against a column while he waited.
No point in offending the fellows who watched
him with hard eyes even when they bellowed
verses in a language he knew only well enough to
recognize.

No wonder Scratchard hadn't been able to make
it to the plaza as he'd intended. The other two
staircases were open and in use, but the procession route certainly extended some distance to
either side of the river; and Scratchard, with business of his own to take care of, would have waited
till the last minute before setting out to collect an
officer returning from furlough.

No problem. But it calmed Tyl to remember
that there *were* other Slammers nearby, in event
of a real emergency.

The gorgeous reliquary was the end of the procession proper. When that reached the heavy doors
at the west end of the mall, a barked order passed
down the lines of guards, repeated by every tenth
man.

The men in white turned and began to double-
time in the direction the procession was headed,
closing up as they moved. They carried their staffs
vertically before them, and their voices boomed a
chant beginning, "Fortis iuventus, virtus audax
bellica. . . . " as they strode away.

They marched in better order than any mercenary unit Tyl could remember having seen—not
that close-order drill was what folks hired the
Slammers for.

And there were a lot of them, for the double
lines continued to shift past and contract for several minutes, more and more quick-stepping staff-
wielders appearing from farther back along the
procession route to the east. They must have timed

their withdrawal so that the whole route would be cleared the instant the procession reached its destination, presumably the cathedral.

At least *something* in this place was organized. It just didn't appear to be what called itself the government.

CHAPTER FIVE

Tyl didn't follow the procession when the route cleared, nor did he try to raise Sergeant-Major Scratchard on his implant again. He'd told Scratchard where he'd be; and if the non-com couldn't find him, then that was important information for Captain Tyl Koopman to know.

There was a surge of civilians—into the mall and through it down the stairs to the plaza—as soon as the procession was clear. Normal folk, so far as Tyl could tell from the loose-fitting fashions current here. Most of them wore a red ribbon or a black one, but there was no contingent of cloaked thugs.

Which meant that the bullies, the enforcers, had gotten word that the main stairs would be blocked when the tide cleared the plaza—although Scratchard and apparently a lot of civilians had been caught unaware. That could mean a lot of

things: none of them particularly good, and none
of them, thank the Lord, the business of Tyl
Koopman or Hammer's Slammers.

He caught sight of a uniform of the right color.

Sergeant Major Scratchard muscled his way
through the crowd, his rank in his eyes and his
grizzled hair. His khaki coveralls were neat and
clean, but there were shiny patches over the shoulders where body armor had rubbed the big man's
uniform against his collarbone.

Tyl hadn't recognized the name, but sight of the
man rang a bell in his mind. He swung away from
the pillar and, gripping the hand the non-com
extended to·him, said, "Sergeant Major Scratchard?
Would that be Ripper Jack?"

Scratchard's professional smile broadened into
something as real and firm as his handshake. "Cap'n
Koopman, then? Yeah, when I was younger,
sir. . . . Maybe when I was younger."

He shifted his right leg and the hand holding
Tyl's, just enough to point without apprising the
civilians around of the gesture.

Scratchard wore a knife along his right calf.
Most of the sheathed blade was hidden within his
boot but the hand-filling grip was strapped to
mid-calf. "Pistols jam on you, happen," the big
man half bragged, half explained. "This'n never
did."

His face hardened. "Though they got me pretty
much retired to Admin now with my bum knees."

"Didn't look that quiet a billet just now," Tyl
said, pitching his voice lower than the civilians,
scurrying on their own errands, could have over-
heard. "Down in the plaza just now, the enforcers
in cloaks. . . . And I was talking to a UDB lieutenant landed the same time I did."

"Yeah, you could maybe figure that," Scratchard said in a voice too quietly controlled to be really neutral. "Open your leg pocket, sir, and stand real close."

Tyl, his face still, ran a finger across the seal of the bellows pocket on the right leg of his coveralls. He and the non-com pressed against one of the door pillars, their backs momentarily to the crowd moving past them. He felt the weight of what Scratchard had slipped into his pocket.

Tyl didn't need to finger the object to know that he'd been given a service pistol, a 1 cm powergun. In the right hands, it could do as much damage as a shotgun loaded with buck.

Tyl's were the right hands. He wouldn't have been in the Slammers if they weren't. But the implications. . .

"We're issuing sidearms in Bamberg City, then?" he asked without any emotional loading.

Scratchard, an enlisted man reporting to an officer, said stiffly, "Sir, while I was in charge of the Transit Detachment, I gave orders that none of the troopers on port leave were to leave barracks in groups of less than three. And no, sidearms aren't officially approved. But I *won't* have men under my charge disarmed when I sure as blazes wouldn't be disarmed myself. You can change the procedures if you like."

"Yes, Sergeant Major, I can," Tyl said with just enough iron to emphasize that he was well aware of their respective ranks. "And if I see any reason to do so, I will."

He smiled, returning the conversation to the footing where he wanted to keep it. "For now, let's get me to the barracks and see just what it is the Colonel has on line."

Pray to the Lord that there'd be orders to take over E Company again.

Scratchard hesitated, looking first toward the east, then the western lock doors. "Ah, sir," he said. "We're billeted in the City Offices—" he pointed toward the eastern end of the mall, the side toward the huge House of Grace. "Central's cut orders for you to carry the Transit Detachment over to Two for further assignment . . . but you know, nothing that can't wait another couple days. We've still got half a dozen other troopers due back from furlough."

"All right," Tyl said, to show that he wasn't going to insist on making a decision before he'd heard Scratchard's appraisal of the situation. "What else?"

"Well, sir," said the non-com. "President Delcorio really wants to see the ranking Slammers officer in the city. Didn't call the message over, his nephew brought it this morning. I told him you were in orbit, due down as soon as the port cleared— 'cause *I'm* bloody not the guy to handle that sort of thing. I checked with Central, see if they'd courier somebody over from Two, but they didn't want. . . ."

Tyl understood why Colonel Hammer would have turned down Scratchard's request. It was obvious what President Delcorio wanted to discuss . . . and it wasn't something that Hammer wanted to make a matter of official regimental policy by sending over a staff officer.

The Slammers hadn't been hired to keep public order in Bamberg City, and Colonel Hammer wanted all the time he could get before he had to officially make a decision that might involve the Bonding Authority either way.

"Central said you should handle it for now," Scratchard concluded. "And I sure think *somebody* ought to report to the President ASAP."

"Via," muttered Tyl Koopman.

Well, he couldn't say that he hadn't been given a responsible job when he returned from furlough.

He shrugged his shoulders, settling the pack more comfortably. "Right," he said. "Let's do it then, Sergeant Major."

"Palace of Government," Scratchard said in evident relief, pointing west in the direction the procession had been headed. He stepped off with a stiff-legged stride that reminded Tyl that the non-com had complained about his knees.

The crowd had thinned enough that the Slammers officer could trust other pedestrians to avoid him even if he glanced away from his direction of movement. "You go by Jack when you're with friends?" he asked, looking at the bigger man.

"Yessir, I do," Scratchard replied.

He grinned, and though the expression wasn't quite natural, the non-com was working on it.

Mercenary units were always outnumbered by the indigenous populations that hired them—or they were hired to put down. Mercenaries depended on better equipment, better training—and on each other, because everything else in the world could be right and you were still dead if the man who should have covered your back let you down.

Tyl and Scratchard both wanted—*needed*—there to be a good relationship between them. It didn't look like they'd be together long . . . but life itself was temporary, and that wasn't a reason not to make things work as well as they could while it lasted.

"This way," said Scratchard as the two soldiers emerged from the mall crossing the river. "Give you a bit of a view, and we don't fight with trucks."

There was a ramp from the mall down to interlocking vehicular streets—one of them paralleling the river, the plaza, and then sweeping west along the corniche. The other was a park-like boulevard which T-ed into the first after separating the gold-domed cathedral from a large, three story building whose wings enclosed a central courtyard open in the direction of the river.

"That's the . . . ?" Tyl said, trying to remember the name.

"Palace of Government, yeah," Scratchard replied easily. He was taking them along the pedestrian walk atop the levee.

Glancing over the railing to his right, Tyl was shocked to see the water was within two meters of the top of the levee. He could climb directly aboard the scores of barges moored there, silently awaiting for the locks to open. All he'd have to do was swing his legs over the guard rail.

"Via!" he said, looking from the river to the street and the buildings beyond it. "What happens if it comes up another couple meters? *All* that down there floods, right?"

"They've got flood shutters on all the lower floors," Scratchard explained/agreed. "They say it happened seventy-odd years ago when everything came together—tides and a storm that backed up the outlet channels up-coast. But they know what they're doing, their engineers."

He paused, then added in a tone of disgust, "Their politicians, now. . . . But I don't suppose they know their asses from a hole in the ground, any of 'em anywhere."

He didn't expect an argument from an officer of Hammer's Slammers; and Tyl Koopman wasn't about to give him one.

Bamberg City was clean, prosperous. The odor of toasted tobacco lead permeated it, despite the fact that the ranks of hogsheads on the waiting barges were all vacuum-sealed; but that was a sweet smell very different from the reeks that were the normal concomitant of bulk agriculture.

Nothing wrong here but the human beings.

A flagpole stood in the courtyard of the Palace of Government. Its twelve-man honor guard wore uniforms of the same blue and gold as the fabric of the drooping banner.

In front of the cathedral were more than a thousand of the men in cross-marked white robes. They were still chanting and blocking vehicles, though the gaps in the ranks of staff-armed choristers permitted pedestrians to enter the cathedral building. The dome towered above this side of the river, though it in turn was dwarfed by the House of Grace opposite.

There was a pedestrian bridge from the embankment to the courtyard of the Palace of Government, crossing the vehicular road. As they joined the traffic on it, heavy because of the way vehicles were being backed up by the tail end of the procession, Tyl asked, "Who wears white here? The ones who hold Easter on Christmas?"

"Umm," said the sergeant major. The non-com's tone reminded Tyl of the pistol that weighted his pocket—and the reason it was there.

In a barely audible voice, Scratchard went on, "Those are orderlies from the House of Grace. They, ah, usually turn out for major religious events."

Neither of the mercenaries spoke again until they had reached the nearly-empty courtyard of the government building. Then, while the honor guard was still out of earshot, Tyl said, "Jack, they don't look to me like they empty bedpans."

"Them?" responded the big sergeant major. "They do whatever Bishop Trimer tells them to do, sir."

He glanced over his shoulder in the direction of the massed orderlies. His eyes held only flat appraisal, as if he were estimating range and the length of the burst he was about to fire.

"Anything at all," he concluded.

Tyl Koopman didn't pursue the matter as he and Scratchard—the latter limping noticeably—walked across the courtyard toward the entrance of the Palace of Government.

He could feel the eyes of the honor guard following them with contempt. It didn't bother him much, any more.

Five years in the Slammers had taught him that parade-ground soldiers always felt that way about killers in uniform.

CHAPTER SIX

The flood shutters of the Palace of Government
were closed, and Charles Desoix wasn't naive
enough to think that the thick steel plates had
been set against the chance of a storm surge.
Bamberg City had really come apart in the two
weeks he was gone.

Or just maybe it was starting to come together,
but President John Delcorio wasn't going to be
part of the new order.

Desoix threw a sharp salute to the head of the
honor guard. The Bamberg officer returned it while
the men of his section presented arms.

Striding with his shoulders back, Desoix proceeded toward the front entrance—the only opening on the first two stories of the palace that
wasn't shuttered.

As Desoix looked at it, the saluting was protec-
tive coloration. It was purely common sense to

want the respect of the people around you . . . and when you've wangled billets for yourself and your men in the comfort of the Palace of Government, that meant getting along with the Executive Guards.

By thumbing an epaulet loop, Desoix brightened the gray-spattered markings of his uniform to metallic silver—and it was easy to learn to salute, as easy as learning to hold the sight picture that would send a bolt of cyan death down-range at a trigger's squeeze. There was no point in not making it easy on yourself.

He thought of making a suggestion to the Slammers officer who'd just arrived, but. . . Tyl Koopman seemed a good sort and as able as one of Colonel Hammer's company commanders could be expected to be.

But Koopman also seemed the sort of man who might be happier with his troops in the police barracks beneath the City Offices than he would be in the ambiance of the Palace.

The captain in command of the guards at the entrance was named Sanchez; he roomed next door to Desoix in the officers' quarters in the West Wing. Instead of saluting again, Desoix took the man's hand and said, "Well, Rene, I'm glad to be back on a civilized planet again . . . but what on *earth* has been going on in the city since I left?"

The Guards captain made a sour face and looked around at the sergeant and ten men of his section. Everyone in the Executive Guard was at least sponsored by one of the top families on the planet. Not a few of them were members of those families, asserting a tradition of service without the potential rigors of being stationed on Two if the Crusade got under way.

"Well, you know the people," Sanchez said, a gentleman speaking among gentlemen. "The recent taxes haven't been popular, since there are rumors that they have more to do with Lady Eunice's wardrobe than with propagation of Christ's message. Nothing that we need worry about."

Desoix raised an eyebrow. The Executive Guards carried assault rifles whose gilding made them as ornamental as the gold brocade on the men's azure uniforms . . . but there were magazines in the rifles today. That was as unusual as the flood shutters being in place.

"Ah, you can't really stay neutral if things get . . . out of hand, can you?" the UDB officer asked. He didn't like to suggest that he and Sanchez were on different standards; but that was better than using "we" when the word might seem to commit the United Defense Batteries.

The guardsman's face chilled. "We'll follow orders, of course," he said. "But it isn't the business of the army to get involved in the squabbles of the mob—or to attempt to change the will of the people."

"Exactly," said Desoix, nodding enthusiastic agreement. "*Exactly.*"

He was still nodding as he strode into the entrance rotunda. He hoped he'd covered his slip with Sanchez well enough.

But he certainly *had* learned where the army—or at least the Executive Guard—stood on the subject of the riots in the streets.

There was a small, separately-guarded, elevator off the rotunda which opened directly onto the Consistory Room on the third floor. Desoix hesitated. The pager inset into his left cuff had lighted red with Major Borodin's anxiety, and Desoix knew what his commander wanted without admitting his presence by answering.

It would be a *very* good idea to take the elevator. Borodin was awkward in the company of President Delcorio and his noble advisors; the major, the battery, and the situation would all benefit from the presence of Lieutenant Charles Desoix.

But Desoix had some personal priorities as well, and. . .

There was traffic up and down the central staircase—servants and minor functionaries, but not as many of them as usual. They had an air of nervousness rather than their normal haughty superiority.

When the door of the small meeting room near the elevator moved, Desoix saw Anne McGill through the opening.

Desoix strode toward her, smiling outwardly and more relieved than he could admit within. He wasn't the type who could ever admit being afraid that a woman wouldn't want to see him again—or that he cared enough about her that it would matter.

The panel, dark wood placed between heavy engaged columns of pink-and-gray marble, closed again when he moved toward it. She'd kept it ajar, watching for his arrival, and had flashed a sight of herself to signal Desoix closer.

But Lady Anne McGill, companion and confidante of the President's wife, had no wish to advertise her presence here in the rotunda.

Desoix tapped on the door. He heard the lock click before the panel opened, hiding Anne behind it from anyone outside. Maybe her ambivalence was part of the attraction, he thought as he stepped into a conference room. There was a small, massively-built table, chairs for six, and space for that many more people to stand if they knew one another well.

All the room held at the moment was the odor of heavy tobaccos, so omnipresent on Bamberia that Desoix noticed it only because he'd been off-planet for two weeks . . . and Anne McGill in layers of silk chiffon which covered her like mist, hiding everything while everything remained suggested.

Desoix put his arms around her.

"Charles, it's very dangerous," she said, turning so that his lips met her cheek.

He nuzzled her ear and, when she caught his right hand, he reached for her breast with his left.

"Ah . . ." he said as a different level of risk occurred to him. "Your husband's still stationed on Two, isn't he?"

"Of course," Anne muttered scornfully.

She was no longer fighting off his hands, but she was relaxing only slightly and that at a subconscious level. "You don't think Bertrand would be *here* when things are like this, do you? There's a Consistory Meeting every morning now, but things are getting worse. *Anyone* can see that. Eunice says that they're all cowards, all the men, even her husband."

She let her lips meet his. Her body gave a shudder and she gripped Desoix to her as fiercely as her tension a moment before had attempted to repel him. "You should be upstairs now," she whispered as she turned her head again. "They need you and your Major, he's very upset."

"My call unit would have told me that if I'd

asked it," the UDB officer said as he shifted the grip of his hands. Anne was a big woman, large-boned and with a tendency toward fat that she repressed fiercely with exercise and various diets. She wore nothing beneath the bottom layer of chiffon except the smooth skin which Desoix caressed. His hand ran up her thigh to squeeze the fat of her buttock against the firm muscle beneath.

"Then don't be long . . ." Anne whispered as she reached for the fly of his trousers.

Desoix didn't know quite what she meant by that.

But he knew that it didn't matter as he backed his mistress against the table, lifting the chiffon dress to spill over the wood where there would be no risk of staining the fabric.

CHAPTER SEVEN

"Captain Tyl Koopman, representing Hammer's Regiment," boomed the greeter, holding the door of the Consistory Room ajar—and blocking Tyl away from it with her body, though without appearing to do so.

"Enter," said someone laconically from within. The greeter swept the panel open with a flourish, bowing to Tyl.

Machines could have done all the same things, Tyl thought with amusement; but they wouldn't have been able to do them with such pomp. Even so, the greeter, a plump woman in an orange and silver gown, was only a hint of the peacock-bright gathering within the Consistory Room.

There were twenty or thirty people, mostly men, within the domed room above the rotunda. Natural lighting through the circumference of arched windows made the Slammers officer blink. It differed in quality (if not necessarily intensity) from the glowstrips in the corridors through which he had been guided to reach the room.

The only men whose garments did not glitter with metallic threads were those whose clothing glowed with internal lambency from powerpacks woven into the seams. President John Delcorio, in black velvet over which a sheen trembled from silver to ultra-violet, was the most striking of the lot.

"Good to see you at last, Captain," Delcorio boomed as if in assurance that Tyl would recognize him—as he did—from the holograms set in niches in the hallways of the Palace of Government. "Maybe your veterans can put some backbone into our own forces, don't you think? So that we can all get down to the real business of cleansing Two for Christ."

He glowered at a middle-aged man whose uniform was probably that of a serving officer, because its dark green was so much less brilliant than what anyone else in the room seemed to be wearing.

John Delcorio was shorter than Tyl had assumed, but he had the chest and physical presence of a big man indeed. His hair, moustache, and short beard were black with gray speckles that were probably works of art: the President was only thirty-two standard years old. He had parlayed his position as Head of Security into the presidency when the previous incumbent, his uncle, died three years before.

Delcorio's eyes sparkled, and the flush on his cheeks was as much ruddy good-health as a vestige of his present anger. Tyl could understand how a man with eyes that sharp could cut his way to leadership of a wealthy planet.

But he could also see how such a man's pushing would bring others to push back, push hard. . . .

Maybe too hard.

"Sir," Tyl replied, wondering what you were *supposed* to call the President of Bamberia when you met him. "I haven't been fully briefed yet on the situation. But Hammer's Slammers carry out their contracts."

He hoped that was neutral enough; and he hoped to the *Lord* that Delcorio would let him drop into the background now.

"Yes, well," said Delcorio. The quick spin of his hand was more or less the dismissal Tyl had hoped for. "Introduce Major Koopman to the others, Thomas. Have something to drink—" There was a well-stocked sideboard beneath one of the windows, and most of those present had glasses in their hands. "We're waiting for Bishop Trimer, you see."

"How *long* are you going to wait before you send for him, John?" asked the woman in the red dress that shimmered like a gasoline flame. She wasn't any taller than the President; but like him, she flashed with authority as eye-catching as her clothes. "You *are* the President, you know."

It struck Tyl that Delcorio and this woman who could only be his wife wore the colors of the Easter factions he had seen at daggers-drawn in the plaza. That made as little sense as anything else in Bamberg City.

"Major, then, is it?" murmured a slender fellow at Tyl's elbow, younger than the mercenary had been when he joined the Slammers. "I'm Thom

Chastain, don't you see, and this is my brother Richie. What would you like to drink?"

"Ah, I'm really just a captain," Tyl said, wondering whether Delcorio had misheard, was being flattering—or was incensed that Hammer had sent only a company commander in response to a summons from his employer. "Ah, I don't think. . ."

"Eunice," the President was saying in a voice like a slap, "this is *scarcely* the time to precipitate disaster by insulting the man who can stabilize the situation."

"The *army* can stabilize—" the woman snapped.

"It isn't the business of the army—" boomed the soldier in green.

The volume of his interruption shocked him as well as the others in the wrangle. All three paused. When the discussion resumed, it was held in voices low enough to be ignored if not unheard.

"Queen Eunice," said Thom Chastain, shaking his head. There was a mixture of affection and amusement in his voice, but Tyl had been in enough tight places to recognize the flash of fear in the young man's eyes. "She's really a terror, isn't she?"

"Ah," Tyl said while his mind searched for a topic that had nothing to do with Colonel Hammer's employers. "You gentlemen are in the army also, I gather?"

There were couches around most of the walls. Near one end was a marble conference table that matched the inlaid panels between the single-sheet vitril windows. Nobody was sitting down, and the groups of two or three talking always seemed to be glancing over their collective shoulders toward the door, waiting for the missing man.

"Oh, well, these," said the other Chastain brother, Richie—surely a twin. He flicked the

collar of his blue and gold uniform, speaking with
the diffidence Tyl had felt at being addressed as
"Major."

"We're honorary colonels in the Guards, you
know," said Thom. "But it's because of our grandfather. We're not very inter. . ."

"Well, Grandfather Chastain was, you know,"
said Richie, taking up where his brother's voice
trailed off. "He was president some years ago.
Esteban Delcorio succeeded him, but Thom and I
are something like colonels for life—"

"—and so we wear—"

They concluded, both together, "But we aren't
soldiers the way you are, Major."

"Or Marshal Dowell, either," Thom Chastain
added later, nodding to the man in green who had
broken away from the Delcorios—leaving them to
hiss at one another. "Now, what would you like to
drink?"

Just about anything, thought Tyl. So long as it
had enough kick to knock him on his ass . . .
which, in a situation like this would get him sacked
if the Colonel didn't decide he should instead be
shot out of hand. Why in *blazes* hadn't somebody
from the staff been couriered over on an "errand"
that left him available to talk informally with the
civil authorities?

"Nothing for me, thank you," Tyl said aloud.
"Or, ah, water?"

Marshal Dowell had fallen in with a tall man
whose clothes were civilian in cut, though they
carried even more metallic brocade than trimmed
the military uniforms. The temporary grouping
broke apart abruptly when Dowell turned away
and the tall man shouted at his back, "No, I *don't*
think that's a practical solution, Marshal! Abdicat-

ing your responsibilities makes it impossible for
me to carry out mine."

"Berne is the City Prefect," Thom whispered
into Tyl's ear. The Chastain brothers were person-
able kids—but "kid" was certainly the word for
them. They *seemed* even younger than their prob-
able age—which was old enough to ride point in
an assault force, in Tyl's terms of reference.

From the other side, Richie was saying, "There's
been a lot of trouble in the streets recently, you
know. Berne keeps saying that he doesn't have
enough police to take care of it."

"It is *not* in the interests of God or the State,"
responded Marshal Dowell, his voice shrill and
his face as red as a flag, "that we give up the
Crusade on Two because of some rabble that the
police would deal with if they were used with
decision!"

Tyl saw a man in uniform staring morosely out
over the city. The uniform was familiar; desire
tricked the Slammers officer into thinking that he
recognized the man as well.

" 'Scuse me," he muttered to the Chastains and
strode across the circular room. "Ah, Lieutenant
Desoix?"

Tyl's swift motion drew all eyes in the room to
him—so he felt/knew that everyone recognized
his embarrassment when the figure in silhouette
at the window turned: a man in his mid forties,
jowls sagging, paunch sagging. . . . Twenty years
older than Charles Desoix and twenty kilos softer.

"Charles?" the older man barked as his eyes
quested the room for the subject of Tyl's call.
"Where have you—"

Then he realized, from the way the Slammers
officer's face went from enthusiastic to stricken,

what had happened. He smiled, an expression that reminded Tyl of snow slumping away from a rocky hillside in the spring, and said, "You'd be Hammer's man? I'm Borodin, got the battery of the UDB here that keeps them all—" he nodded toward nothing in particular, pursing his lips to make the gesture encompass everyone in the room "—safe in their beds."

The scowl with which Major Borodin followed the statement made a number of the richly-dressed Bamberg officials turn their interest to other parts of the room.

Tyl was too concerned with controlling his own face to worry about the reason for Borodin's anger— which was explained when the UDB officer continued, "I gather we're looking for the same man. And I must say, if *you* could get down from orbit in time to be here, I don't understand what Charles' problem can be."

"He—" said Tyl. Then he smiled brightly and replaced his intended statement with, "I'm sure Lieutenant Desoix will be here as soon as possible. It's very—difficult out there, getting around, it seems to me."

"Tell me about it, boy," Borodin grunted as he turned again to the window, not so much rude as abstracted.

They were looking out over the third-story porch which faced the front of the Palace of Government. In the courtyard below were the foreshortened honor guard and the flag, still drooping and unrecognizable. The river beyond was visible only by inference. Its water, choked between the massive levees, was covered with barges ten and twelve abreast, waiting to be passed through beneath the plaza.

On the other side of the river—

"That's the City Offices, then?" Tyl asked.

Where he and the men under his temporary
charge were billeted. And where now police vehicles swarmed, disgorging patrolmen and comatose
prisoners in amazing numbers.

"Claims to be," Borodin grunted. "Don't see
much sign that anything's being run from there,
do you?"

He glanced around. He was aware enough of
his surroundings to make sure that nobody but the
other mercenary officer would overhear the next
comment. "Or from here, you could bloody well
say."

The door opened. The scattered crowd in the
Consistory Room turned toward the sound with
the sudden unanimity of a school of fish changing
front.

"Father Laughlin, representing the Church,"
called the greeter in a clear voice that left its
message unmistakable.

The President's face settled as if he had just
watched one wing of the building crumble away.
Eunice Delcorio swore like a transportation sergeant.

"Wait out here, boys," said a huge man—soft-
looking but not far short of two meters in height—in
white priestly vestments. "You won't be needed."

He was speaking, Tyl saw through the open
door, to a quartet of "hospital orderlies." They
looked even more like shock troops than they had
in the street, though these weren't carrying their
staffs.

Eunice Delcorio swore again. The skin over her
broad cheekbones had gone sallow with rage.

Father Laughlin appeared to be at ease and in

perfect control of himself, but Tyl noticed that the priest ducked instinctively when he entered the room—though he would have had to be a full meter taller to bump his head on any of the lintels in the Palace of Government.

"Where's Trimer?" Delcorio demanded in a voice that climbed a note despite an evident attempt to control it.

"Bishop Trimer, you—" Laughlin began smoothly.

"Where's Trimer?"

"Holding a Service of Prayer for Harmony in the cathedral," the priest said, no longer trying to hide the ragged edges of emotion behind an unctuous wall.

"He was told to be here!" said Berne, the City Prefect, breaking into the conversation because he was too overwhelmed by his own concerns to leave the matter to the President. He stepped toward the priest, his green jacket fluttering—a rangy mongrel snarling at a fat mastiff which will certainly make a meal of it should the mastiff deign to try.

"Bishop Trimer appreciated the President's invitation," Laughlin said, turning and nodding courteously toward Delcorio. "He sent me in response to it. He was gracious enough to tell me that he had full confidence in my ability to report your concerns to him. But his first duty is to the Church—and to all members of his flock, rather than to the secular authorities who have their own duties."

The Chastain brothers were typical of those in the Consistory Room, men of good family gathered around the President not so much for their technical abilities but because they controlled large blocks of wealth and personnel on their estates. They watched from the edges of the room with the fascination of spectators at a bloody accident, saying nothing and looking away whenever the eyes of one of the principals glanced across them.

"All right," said Eunice Delcorio to her husband. Her eyes were as calm as the crust on a pool of lava. "Now you've got to recall troops. Tell him."

She pointed toward Marshal Dowell scorning to look at the military commander directly.

"Your will, madam—" Dowell began with evident dislike.

"My *will* is that you station two regiments in the city at once, Marshal Dowell," Eunice Delcorio said with a voice that crackled like liquid oxygen flowing through a field of glass needles. "Or that you wait in the cells across the river until some successor of my husband chooses to release you."

"With your leave, sir," Dowell huffed in the direction of the President.

The Marshal was angry now, and it wasn't the earlier flashing of someone playing dangerous political games with his peers. He was lapsing into the normal frustration of a professional faced with laymen who didn't understand why he couldn't do something they thought was reasonable.

"Madam," Dowell continued with a bow to Eunice Delcorio, "your will impresses me, but it doesn't magically make transport for three thousand men and their equipment available on Two. It doesn't provide rations and accommodations for them here. And if executed with no more consideration than I've been able to give it in this room, away from my staff, it will almost certainly precipitate the very disasters that concern you.

"You—" Dowell went on.

"You—" Eunice Delcorio snapped.

"You—" the City Prefect shouted.

"You—" Father Laughlin interrupted weightily.

"You will all be silent!" said John Delcorio, and though the President did not appear to raise his voice to an exceptional level, none of the angry people squabbling in front of him continued to speak.

The two mercenary officers exchanged glances. It had occurred to both of them that any situation was salvageable if the man in charge retained the poise that President Delcorio was showing now.

"Gentlemen, Eunice," Delcorio said, articulating the thought the mercenaries had formed. "We are the *government*, not a mob of street brawlers. So long as we conduct ourselves calmly but firmly, this minor storm will be weathered and we will return to ordinary business."

He nodded to the priest. "And to the business of God, to the Crusade on Two. Father Laughlin, I trust that Bishop Trimer will take *all* necessary precautions to prevent his name from being used by those who wish to stir up trouble?"

Delcorio's voice was calm, but nobody in the room doubted how intense the reaction might be if the priest did not respond properly.

"Of course, President Delcorio," Laughlin said, bowing low.

There was a slight motion on the western edge of the room as a door opened to pass a big woman floating in a gown of white chiffon. She wasn't announced by a greeter, and she made very little stir at this juncture in the proceedings as she slipped through the room to stand near Eunice Delcorio.

"Lord Berne," Delcorio continued to his tall prefect, "I expect your police to take prompt, firm action wherever trouble erupts." His eyes were piercing.

"Yes sir," Berne said, his willing enthusiasm pinned by his master's fierce gaze. Alone of the civilians in the room, he owed everything he had to his position in the government. The richness of his garments showed just how much he had acquired in that time.

"I've already done that," he explained. "I've canceled leaves and my men have orders that all brawling is to be met with overwhelming force and the prisoners jailed. I've suspended normal release procedures for the duration of the emergency also."

Berne hesitated as the implications of what he had just announced struck him anew. "Ah, in accordance with your previous directions, sir. And your assurance that additional support would be available from the army as required."

Nobody spoke. The President nodded as he turned slowly to his military commander and said, "Marshal, I expect you to prepare for the transfer of two regular regiments back to the vicinity of the capital."

Dowell did not protest, but his lips pursed.

"*Prepare*, Marshal," Delcorio repeated harshly. "Or do you intend to inform me that you're no longer fit to perform your duties?"

"Sir," Dowell said. "As you order, of course."

"And you will further coordinate with the City Prefect so that the Executive Guard is ready to support the police if and when I order it?"

Not a command but a question, and a fierce

promise of what would happen if the wrong answer were given.

"Yes sir," Marshal Dowell repeated. "As you order." Berne was nodding and rubbing his hands together as if trying to return life to them after a severe chill.

"Then, gentlemen . . ." Delcorio said, with warmth and a smile as engaging as his visage moments before had threatened. "I believe we can dismiss this gathering. Father Laughlin, convey my regrets to the Bishop that he couldn't be present, but that I trust implicitly his judgment as to how best to return civil life to its normal calm."

The priest bowed again and turned toward the door. He was not the same man in demeanor as the one who had entered the meeting, emphasizing his importance by blatantly displaying his bodyguards.

"Praise the Lord," Tyl muttered, more to himself than to Major Borodin. "I've been a lotta places I liked better 'n this one—and some of them, people were shooting at me."

Nodding to take his leave of the UDB officer, Tyl started for the door that was already being opened from the outside.

"Lieutenant Desoix of United Defense Batteries," the greeter announced.

"You there," Eunice Delcorio called in a throaty contralto—much less shrill than her previous words had led Tyl to imagine her ordinary voice would be. "Captain Koopman. Wait a moment."

Father Laughlin was already out of the room. Borodin was bearing down on his subordinate with obvious wrath that Desoix prepared to meet with a wry smile.

Everybody else looked at Tyl Koopman.

She'd gotten his name and rank right, he thought as his skin flashed hot and his mind stumbled over itself wondering what to say, what she wanted, and why in *blazes* Colonel Hammer had put him in this bucket. He was a *line* officer and this was a job for the bloody staff!

"Yes, ma'am," he said aloud, turning toward his questioner. His eyes weren't focusing right because of the unfamiliar strain, so he was seeing the president's wife as a fiery blur beneath an imperious expression.

"How many men are there under your command, Captain?" Eunice continued. There was no hostility in her voice, only appraisal. It was the situation that was freezing Tyl's heart—having to answer questions on this level, rather than the way in which the questions were being asked.

"Ma'am, ah?" he said. What had Scratchard told him as they walked along the levee? "Ma'am, there's about a hundred men here. That's twenty or so in the base establishment, and the rest the transit unit that, you know, I'll be taking to Two in a few days."

"No," the woman said, coolly but in a voice that didn't even consider the possibility of opposition. "We certainly aren't sending any troops *away*, now."

"Yes, that's right," Delcorio agreed.

A tic brushed the left side of the President's face. The calm with which he had concluded the meeting was based on everything going precisely as he had choreographed it in his mind. Eunice was adding something to the equation, and even something as minor as that was dangerous to his state of mind if he hadn't foreseen it.

"Ah . . ." said Tyl. "I'll need to check with Cen—"

"Well, *do* it, then!" Delcorio blazed. "Do I need to be bothered with details that a *corporal* ought to be able to deal with?"

"Yes *sir!*" said the Slammers officer.

He threw the President a salute because it felt right.

And because that was a good opening to spinning on his heel and striding rapidly toward the door, on his way *out* of this room.

CHAPTER EIGHT

Headquarters and billets for the enlisted men of Battery D were in a basement room of the Palace of Government, converted to the purpose from a disused workers' cafeteria. Desoix sighed to see it again, knowing that here his superior would let out the anger he had bottled up while the two of them stalked through hallways roamed by folk from outside the unit.

Control, the artificial intelligence/communications center, sat beside a wall that had been pierced for conduits to antennas on the roof. It was about a cubic meter of electronics packed into thirty-two resin-black modules, some of them redundant.

Control directed the battery in combat because no human reactions were fast enough to deal with hypersonic missiles—though the calliopes, pulsing with light-swift violence, could rip even those from the sky if their tubes were slewed in the right direction.

The disused fixtures were piled at one end of
the room. Control's waste heat made the room a
little warmer, a little drier; but the place still
reminded Desoix of basements in too many bombed-
out cities.

Major Borodin pulled shut the flap of the curtain which separated his office from the bunks on
which the off-duty shift was relaxing or trying to
sleep. In theory, the curtain's microprocessors
formed adaptive ripples in the fabric and canceled
sounds. In practice—

Well, it didn't work that badly. And if you're
running an eighty-man unit in what now had to be
considered combat conditions, you'd better figure
your troops were going to learn what was going on
no matter how you tried to conceal it.

"You should have called in at once!" the battery
commander said, half furious, half disappointed,
like a parent whose daughter has come home three
hours later than expected.

"I needed you at that meeting," he added, the
anger replaced by desperate memory. "I . . . you
know, Charles, I never know what to say to them
up there. We're supposed to be defending the air
space here, not mixed up in riots."

"I got a good look at that this morning, Sergei,"
Desoix said quietly. He seated himself carefully
on the collapsible desk and, by his example, urged
Borodin into the only chair in the curtained-off
corner. "I think we need to reposition Gun Three.
It's too close to where—things are going on. Some
of our people are going to get hurt."

Borodin shook his craggy head abruptly. "We
can't do that," he said. "Coverage."

"Now that Five's back on-planet—" Desoix began.

"You were with that woman, weren't you?"
Borodin said, anger hardening his face as if it were

concrete setting. "That's really why you didn't come to me when I needed you. I *saw* her slip in just before you did."

Yes, Daddy, Desoix thought. But Borodin was a good man to work for—good enough to humor.

"Sergei," he said calmly, "now that we've got a full battery again, I can readjust coverage areas. We can handle the seafront from the suburbs east and west, I'm pretty—"

"Charles, you're going to get into really terrible trouble," Borodin continued, his voice now sepulchral. "Get us all into trouble."

He looked up at his subordinate and added, "Now, I was younger too, I understand. . . . But believe me, boy, there's plenty of it going around on a businesslike basis. And that's a *curst* sight safer."

Desoix found himself getting angry—and that made him even angrier, at himself, because it meant that Anne mattered to him.

Who you screwed wasn't nearly as dangerous as caring about her.

"Look," he said, hiding the edge in his voice but unable to eliminate the tremble. "I just shook a calliope loose on Merrinet, and it cost the unit less than three grand plus my transportation. I *solve* pro—"

"You paid a fine?"

"Via, no! I didn't pay a fine," Desoix snapped.

Shifting into a frustrated and disappointed tone of his own—a good tactic in this conversation, but exactly the way Desoix was really feeling at the moment also—he continued, "Look, Sergei, I bribed the Customs inspectors to switch manifests. The gun was still being held in the transit warehouse, there wasn't a police locker big enough for a calliope crated for shipment. If I'd pleaded it through the courts, the gun would be on Merrinet when we were old and gray. I—"

He paused, struck by a sudden rush of empathy for the older man.

Borodin was a fine combat officer and smart enough to find someone like Charles Desoix to handle the subtleties of administration that the major himself could never manage. But though he functioned ably as battery commander, he was as lost in the job's intricacies as a man in a snowstorm. Having an executive officer to guide him made things safe—until they weren't safe, and he wouldn't know about the precipice until he plunged over it.

Desoix was just as lost in the way he felt about Lady Anne McGill; and, unlike Borodin, he didn't even have a guide.

He gripped Borodin's hand. "Sergei," he said, "I won't ask you to trust me. But I'll ask you to trust me not to do anything that'll hurt the battery. All right?"

Their eyes met. Borodin's face worked in a moue that was as close to assent as he was constitutionally able to give to the proposition.

"Then let's get back to business," Charles Desoix said with a bright smile. "We need to get a crew to Gun Five for set-up, and then we'll have to juggle duty rosters for permanent manning—unless we can get Operations to send us half a dozen men from Two to bring us closer to strength."

Borodin was nodding happily as his subordinate outlined ordinary problems with ordinary solutions.

Desoix just wished that he could submerge his own concerns about what he was doing.

CHAPTER NINE

"Locked on," said the mechanical voice of Command Central in Tyl's ears. "Hold f—"

There was a wash of static as the adaptive optics of the satellite failed to respond quickly enough to a disturbance in the upper atmosphere.

"—or soft input," continued the voice from Colonel Hammer's headquarters, the words delayed in orbit while the antenna corrected itself.

The air on top of the City Office building was still stirred by the fans of air cars moving to and from the parking area behind. Their numbers had dropped off sharply since the last remnants of the riot were dispersed. In the twilight, it was easier to smell the saltiness from the nearby sea—or else the breezes three stories up carried scents trapped in the alleys lower down.

The bright static across Tyl's screen coalesced into a face, recognizable as a woman wearing a

commo helmet like Tyl's own. Noise popped in
his earphones for almost a second while her lips
moved on the screen—the transmissions were at
slightly different frequencies. Then her voice said,
"Captain Koopman, how secure are these communications on your end?"

"Ma'am?" Tyl said, too recently back from furlough not to treat the communicator as a woman
instead of an enlisted man. "I'm using a portable
laser from the top of the police station. It's—I
think it's pretty safe, but if the signal's a problem,
I can use—"

"Hold one, Captain," the communicator said
with a grin of sorts. Her visage blanked momentarily in static again.

A forest of antennas shared the roof of the building with the Slammers officer: local, regional, and
satellite communications gear. Instead of borrow-
ing a console within to call Central, Tyl squatted
on gritty concrete.

His ten-kilo unit included a small screen, a 20
centimeter rectenna that did its best to align itself
with Hammer's satellites above, and a laser trans-
mitting unit which probably sent Central as fuzzy
a signal as Tyl's equipment managed to receive.

But you can't borrow commo without expecting
the folks who loaned it to be listening in; and if
Tyl did have to stay in Bamberg City with the
transit detachment, he didn't want the locals to
know that he'd been begging Central to withdraw
him.

The screen darkened into a man's face. "Captain Koopman?" said the voice in his helmet. "I
appreciate your sense of timing. I'm glad to have
an experienced officer overseeing the situation there
at the moment."

"Sir!" Tyl said, throwing a salute that was probably out of the restricted field of the pick-up lens.

"Give me your appraisal of the situation, Captain," said the voice of Colonel Alois Hammer. His flat-surface image wobbled according to the vagaries of the upper atmosphere.

"At the moment . . ." Tyl said. He looked away from the screen in an unconscious gesture to gain some time for his thoughts.

The House of Grace towered above him. At the top of the high wall was the visage of Bishop Trimer enthroned. The prelate's eyes were as hard as the stone in which they were carved.

"At the moment, sir, it's quiet," Tyl said to the screen. "The police cracked down hard, arrested about fifty people. Since then—"

"Leaders?" interrupted the helmet in its crackling reproduction of the Colonel's voice. Hammer's eyes were like light-struck diamonds, never dull—never quite the same.

"Brawlers, street toughs," Tyl said contemptuously. "A lot of 'em, is all. But it's been quiet, and. . ."

He paused because he wasn't sure how far he ought to stick his neck out with no data, not really—but his commanding officer waited expectantly on the other end of the satellite link.

"Sir," Tyl said, determined to do the job he'd been set, even though this stuff scared him in a different way from a firefight. There he *knew* what he was supposed to do. "Sir, I haven't been here long enough to know what's normal, but the way it feels out there now. . ."

He looked past the corner of the hospital building and down into the plaza. Many of the booths were still set up and a few were lighted—but not nearly enough to account for the numbers of people gathering there in the twilight. It was like watching gas pool in low spots, mixing and waiting for the spark that would explode it.

"The only places I been that felt like this city does now are night positions just before somebody hits us."

"Rate the players, Captain," said Hammer's voice as his face on the screen flickered and dimmed with the lights of an air car whining past, closer to the roof than it should have been for safety.

The vehicle was headed toward the plaza. Its red and white emergency flashers were on, but the car's idling pace suggested that they were only a warning.

As if *he* knew anything about this sort of thing, Tyl thought bitterly. But the Colonel was right, he could give the same sort of assessment that any mercenary officer learned to do of the local troops he was assigned to support. It didn't really matter that these weren't wearing uniforms.

Some of them weren't wearing uniforms.

"Delcorio's hard but he's brittle," Tyl said aloud. "He'd do all right with enough staff to take the big shocks, but what he's got. . ."

He paused, collecting his thoughts further. Hammer did not interrupt, but the fluctuation of his image on the little screen reminded Tyl that time was passing.

"All right," the Slammers captain continued. "The police, they seem to be holding up pretty well. Berne, the City Prefect, don't have any friends and I don't guess much support. On that end, it's gone about as far as it can and keep the lid on."

Hammer was nodding, but Tyl ignored that too. He had his data marshaled, now, and he needed to spit things out while they were clear to him. "The army, Dowell at least, he's afraid to move and he's not afraid not to move. He won't push anything himself, but Delcorio won't get much help from there.

"And the rest of 'em, the staff—" Tyl couldn't think of the word the group had been called here "—they're nothing, old men and young kids, nobody that matters . . . ah, except the wife, you know, sir? Ah, Lady Eunice. Only she wants to push harder than I think they can push here with what they got and what they got against 'em."

"The mob?" prompted the Colonel. Static added a hiss to words without sibilants.

Tyl looked toward the plaza. The sky was still blue over the western horizon, behind the cathedral's dome and the Palace of Government. The sunken triangle of the plaza was as dark as a volcano's maw, lighted only by the sparks of lanterns and apparently open flames.

"Naw, not the mobs," Tyl said, letting his helmet direct his voice while his eyes gathered data instead of blinking toward his superior. "Them, they'd handle each other if it wasn't any more. But—"

He looked up. The sunset slid at an angle across the side of the House of Grace. The eyes of Bishop Trimer's carven face were as red as blood.

"Sir," Tyl blurted, "it's the Church behind it, the Bishop, and he's going to walk off with the whole thing soon unless Delcorio's luckier 'n anybody's got a right to expect. I think—"

No, say it right.

"Sir," he said, "I recommend that all regimental forces be withdrawn from Bamberg City at once, to avoid us being caught up in internal fighting.

There are surface-effect freighters at the port right
now. With your authorization, I'll charter one immediately and have the unit out of here in three
hours."

Two hours, unless he misjudged the willingness
and efficiency of the sergeant major; but he'd promise what he was sure of and surprise people later
by bettering the offer if he could.

Hammer's lips moved. Tyl thought that the words
were delayed by turbulence, but the Colonel was
only weighing what he was about to say before he
put it into audible syllables. After a moment, the
voice and fuzzy screen said in unison, "Captain,
I'm going to tell you what my problem is."

Tyl's lungs filled again. He'd been holding his
breath unknowingly, terrified that his colonel was
about to strip him of his rank for saying too much,
saying the wrong thing. Anything else, that was all
right. . . .

Even command problems that weren't any business of a captain in the line.

"Our contract," Hammer said carefully, "is with
the government of Bamberia, not precisely with
President Delcorio."

The image of the screen glared as if reading on
Tyl's face the interjection his subordinate would
never have spoken aloud. "The difference is the
sort that only matters in formal proceedings—like
a forfeiture hearing before the Bonding Authority, determining whether or not the Regiment has
upheld its end of the contract."

"Yes *sir!*" Tyl said.

Hammer's face lost its hard lines. For a moment, Tyl thought that the hint of grayness was
more than merely an artifact of the degraded signal.

"There's a complication," the Colonel said with

a precision that erased all emotional content from the statement. "Bishop Trimer has been in contact with the Eaglewing Division regarding taking over conduct of the Crusade in event of a change of government."

He shrugged. "My sources," he added needlessly. "It's a small community, in a way."

Then, with renewed force and no hint of the fatigue of moments before, Hammer went on, "In event of Trimer taking over, as you accurately estimated was his intention, we're out of work. That's not the end of the world, and I *certainly* don't want any of my men sacrificed pointlessly—"

"No *sir*," Tyl barked in response to the fierceness in his commander's face.

"—but I need to know whether a functional company like yours might be able to give Delcorio the edge he needs."

Hammer's voice asked, but his eyes demanded. "Stiffen Dowell's spine, give Trimer enough of a wild card to keep him from making his move before the Crusade gets under way and whoever's in charge won't be able to replace units that're already engaged."

And do it, Tyl realized, without a major troop movement that could be called a contract violation by Colonel Hammer, acting against the interests of a faction of his employers.

It might make a junior captain—acting on his own initiative—guilty of mutiny, of course.

"Sir," Tyl said crisply, vibrant to know that he had orders now that he could understand and execute. "We'll do the job if it can be done. Ripper Jack's a good man, cursed good. I don't know the others yet, most of 'em, but it's three-quarters veterans back from furlough and only a few newbie recruits coming in."

"Understand me, Captain," Hammer said—again fiercely. "I *don't* want you to become engaged in fighting unless it's necessary for your own safety. There aren't enough of you to make any difference if the lid really comes off, and I *won't* throw away good men just to save a contract. But if your being in the capital keeps President Delcorio in power for another two weeks . . . ?"

"Yes *sir!*" Tyl repeated brightly, marveling that his commander seemed relieved at his reaction. Via, he was an officer of Hammer's Slammers, wasn't he? Of *course* he'd be willing to carry out orders that were perfectly clear—or as clear as combat orders ever could be.

Keep the men in battle dress and real visible; hint to Dowell that there was a company of panzers waiting just over the horizon to land and *really* kick butt as soon as he said the word. Make waves at the staff meetings. They couldn't bother him now with their manners and fancy clothes.

The Colonel had told Tyl Koopman what to do, and a few rich fops weren't going to affect the way he did it.

"Then carry on, Captain," Hammer said with a punctuation of static in the middle of the words that did not disguise the pleasure in his voice. "There's a lot—"

The sky was a lighter gray than the ground or the sea, but the sun had fully set. The cyan flash of a powergun lanced the darkness like a scream in silence.

"Hold!" Tyl shouted to his superior, rising from his crouch to get a better view past the microwave dish beside him.

A volley of bolts spat from at least half a dozen locations in the plaza. The orbiting police air car staggered and lifted away. Its plastic hull had been hit. The driver's desperate attempt to increase speed fanned the flames to sluggish life; a trail of smoke marked the vehicle's path.

A huge roar came from the crowd in the plaza. Led by a line of torches and lightwands, it crawled like a living thing up both the central and eastern stairs.

They weren't headed for the Palace of Government across the river. They were coming here.

Tyl flipped his helmet's manual switch to the company frequency. "Sar'ent Major," he snapped, "all men in combat gear and ready t' move *soonest!* Three days rations and all the ammo we can carry."

He switched back to the satellite push and began folding the screen—not essential to the transmission—while the face of Colonel Alois Hammer still glowed on it with tigerish intensity.

"Sir," Tyl said without any emotion to waste on the way he was closing his report, "I'll tell you more when I know more."

Then he collapsed the transceiver antenna. Hammer didn't have anything as important to say as the mob did.

CHAPTER TEN

The mob was pulsing toward the City Offices like the two heads of a flood surge. Powergun bolts spiked out of the mass, some aimed at policemen but many were fired at random.

That was the natural reaction of people with the opportunity to destroy something—an ability which carries its own imperatives. Tyl wasn't too worried about that, not if he had his men armed and equipped before they and the mob collided.

But when he clumped down the stairs from the trap door in the roof, he threw a glance over his shoulder. The north doors of the House of Grace had opened, disgorging men who marched in ground-shaking unison as they sang a Latin hymn.

That was real bad for President Delcorio, for Colonel Hammer's chances of retaining his contract—

And possibly real bad for Tyl Koopman and the troops in his charge.

The transit detachment was billeted on the second floor, in what was normally the turn-out room. Temporary bunks, three-high, meant the troops on the top layer couldn't sit up without bumping the ceiling. What floor-space the bunks didn't fill was covered by the foot-lockers holding the troops' personal gear.

Now most of the lockers had been flung open and stood in the disarray left by soldiers trying to grab one last valuable—a watch; a holo projector; a letter. They knew they might never see their gear again.

For that matter, they knew that the gear was about as likely to survive the night as they themselves were—but you had to act as if you *were* going to make it.

Sergeant Major Scratchard stumped among the few troopers still in the bunk room, slapping them with a hand that rang on their ceramic helmets. "Move!" he bellowed with each blow. "It's yer *butts!*"

If the soldier still hesitated with a fitting or to grab for one more bit of paraphernalia, Scratchard gripped his shoulder and spun him toward the door. As Tyl stuck his head into the room, a female soldier with a picture of her father crashed off the jamb beside him, cursing in a voice that was a weapon itself.

"All clear, sir," Scratchard said as the last pair of troopers scampered for the door ahead of him, geese waddling ahead of a keeper with a ready switch. "Kekkonan's running the arms locker, he's a good man."

Tyl used the pause to fold the dish antenna of

his laser communicator. The sergeant major glanced at him. He said in a voice as firm and dismissing as the one he'd been using on his subordinates, "Dump that now. We don't have time fer it."

"I'll gather 'em up outside," Tyl said. "You send 'em down to me, Jack."

He clipped the communicator to his equipment belt. Alone of the detachment, he didn't have body armor. Couldn't worry about that now.

The arms locker, converted from an interrogation room, was next door to the bunk room. The hall was crowded with troopers waiting to be issued weapons and those pushing past, down the stairs with armloads of lethal hardware that they would organize in the street were there was more space.

Tyl joined the queue thumping its way downstairs. As he did so, he glanced over his shoulder and called, "We'll *have* time, Sar'ent Major. And by the Lord! we'll have a secure link to Central when we do."

CHAPTER ELEVEN

For a moment, the exterior of the City Offices was lighted by wall sconces as usual. A second or two after Tyl stepped from the door into bulk of his troops, crouching as they awaited orders, the sconces, the interior lights, and all the street lights visible on the east side of the river switched off.

There was an explosion louder than the occasional popping of slug-throwers in the distance. A transformer installation had been blown up or shorted into self-destruction.

That made the flames, already painting the low clouds pink, more visible.

A recruit turned on his hand light. The veteran beside him snarled, "Fuckhead! Use infra-red on your helmet shield!"

The trooper on the recruit's other side—more direct—slapped the light away and crushed it beneath her boot.

"Sergeants to me," Tyl ordered on the unit push. He flashed momentarily the miniature lightwand that he carried clipped to a breast pocket—for reading and for situations like this, when his troops needed to know where he was.

Even at the risk of drawing fire when he showed them.

He hadn't called for non-coms, because the men here were mostly veterans with a minimum of the five-years service that qualified them for furlough. Seven sergeants crawled forward, about what Tyl had expected and enough for his purposes.

"Twelve-man squads," he ordered, using his commo helmet instead of speaking directly to the cluster of sergeants. That way all his troops would know what was happening.

As much as Tyl did himself, at any rate.

"Gather 'em fast, no screwing around. We're going to move as soon as everybody's clear." He looked at the sergeants, their faceshields down, just as his was—a collection of emotionless balls, and all of them probably as worried as he was: worried about what they knew was coming, and more nervous yet about all the things that *might* happen in darkness, when nobody at all knew which end was up.

"And no shooting, troopers. Unless we got to."

If they had to shoot their way out, they were well and truly screwed. Just as Colonel Hammer had said—there weren't enough of them to matter a fart in a whirlwind if it came down to that.

A pair of emergency vehicles—fire trucks swaying with the weight of the water on board them—roared south along the river toward the City Offices. A huge block of masonry hurtled from the roof of an apartment building just up the street. Tyl saw its arc silhouetted against the pink sky for a moment.

The stone hit the street with a crash and half-bounced, half-rolled, into the path of the lead truck. The fire vehicle slewed to the side, but its wheels weren't adequate to stabilize the kiloliters of water in its ready-use tank. The truck went over and skidded, rotating on its side in sparks and the scream of tortured metal—even before its consort rammed it from behind.

Someone began to fire a slug-thrower from the roof. The trucks were not burning yet, but a stray breeze brought the raw, familiar odor of petroleum fuel to the hunching Slammers.

There wasn't anything in Hell worse than street-fighting in somebody else's city—

And Tyl, like most of the veterans with him, had done it often enough to be sure of that.

A clot of soldiers stumbled out the doorway. Scratchard was the last, unrecognizable for a moment because of the huge load of equipment he carried.

Looked as if he'd staggered out with everything the rest of the company had left in the arms locker, Tyl thought. A veteran like Jack Scratchard should've known to—

Reinforced windows blew out of the second floor with a cyan flash, a bang, and a deep orange *whoom!* that was simultaneously a sound and a vision. The sergeant major hadn't tried to empty the arms locker after all.

"Put this on, sir," Scratchard muttered to the captain as the fire trucks up the street ignited in the spray of burning fragments hurled from the demolition of the Slammers' excess stores. The actinics of the powergun ammunition detonating in its storage containers made exposed skin prickle, but the exploding gasoline pushed at the crouching men with a warm, stinking hand.

Roof floodlights, driven by the emergency generator in the basement, flared momentarily around the City Offices. Shadows pooled beneath the waiting troops. They cursed and ducked lower—or twisted to aim at the lights revealing them.

Volleys of shots from the mob shattered the lenses before any of the Slammers made up their minds to shoot. The twin pincers, from the plaza and from the House of Grace, were already beginning to envelope the office building.

The route north and away was awash in blazing fuel. The police air car that roared off that way, whipping the flames with its vectored thrust, pitched bow-up and stalled as an automatic weapon ranked it from the same roof as the falling masonry had come.

Scratchard had brought a suit of clamshell body armor for Tyl to wear—and a submachinegun to carry along with a bandolier holding five hundred rounds of ammo in loaded magazines.

"We're crossing the river," Tyl said in a voice that barely danced on the spikes of his present consciousness. "By squad."

He hadn't gotten around to numbering the squads. There was a clacking sound as the sergeant major latched Tyl's armor for him.

Tyl pointed at one of the sergeants—he didn't know *any* bloody names!—with his lightwand. "You first. And you. Next—"

In the pause, uncertain in the backlit darkness where the other non-coms were, Scratchard broke in on the command frequency saying, "Haskins, third. Hu, Pescaro, Bogue and Hagemann. *Move*, you dickheads!"

Off the radio, his head close to Tyl's as the captain clipped his sling reflexively to the epaulet tab of his armor and shrugged the heavy bandolier over the opposite shoulder, the sergeant major added, "You lead 'em, sir—I'll hustle their butts from here."

Even as Tyl opened his mouth to frame a reply, Scratchard barked at one of the men who'd appeared just ahead of him, "Kekkonan—you give 'im a hand with names if he needs it, right?"

Sergeant Kekkonan, short and built like one of the tanks he'd commanded, clapped Tyl on the shoulder hard enough that it was just as well the captain had already started in the direction of the thrust—toward the river and the squad running toward the levee wall as swiftly as their load of weapons and munitions permitted.

A column of men came around the northern corner of the building. Their white tunics rippled orange in the glare of the burning vehicles. The leaders carried staffs as they had when they guarded the procession route, but in the next rank back winked the iridium barrels of powerguns and the antennas of sophisticated communications gear.

They were no more than three steps from the nearest of the nervous Slammers. When the leading orderlies shouted and threw themselves out of the way, there were almost as many guns pointed at the troops as pointed by them.

"*Hold!*" Tyl Koopman ordered through his commo helmet as his skin chilled and his face went stiff. Almost they'd made it, but now—

He was running toward the mob of orderlies—

Via! *They* weren't a mob!—with his hands raised, palms forward.

"This isn't our fight!" he cried, hoping he was close enough to the orderlies to be understood by them as well as by the troops on his unit push. "Squads, keep moving—over the levee!"

The column of orderlies had stopped and flattened like the troops they were facing, but there were three men erect at the new head of the line. One carried a shoulder-pack radio; one a bull-horn; and the man in the middle was a priest with a crucifix large enough to be the standard that the whole column followed.

Tyl looked at the priest, wondering if he could grab the butt of his slung weapon fast enough to take some of them with him if the words the priest murmured to the man with the bull-horn brought a blast of shots from the guns aimed at the Slammers captain.

The burning trucks roared. Sealed parts ruptured with plosive sounds and an occasional sharp crack.

"Go on, get out of here," the bull-horn snarled, its crude amplification making the words even harsher than they were when they came from the orderly's throat.

Tyl spun and brandished his lightwand. "Third Squad," he ordered. "Move!"

A dozen of his troopers picked themselves up from the ground and shambled across the street behind him—toward the guns leveled on the mob from the levee's top. The first two squads were deployed there with the advantages of height and a modicum of cover if any of the locals needed a lesson about what it meant to take on Hammer's Slammers.

Tyl's timing hadn't been quite as bad as he'd thought. Hard to tell just what might have happened if the column from the House of Grace had arrived before Tyl's company had a base of fire across the street.

Two more squads were moving together. The leaders of the mob's other arm, bawling their way up the river road, had already reached the south corner of the City Offices. The cries of *"Freedom! Freedom!"* were suddenly punctuated with screams as a dozen or so of the leaders collapsed under a burst of electrostatic needles fired by one of the policemen inside.

Tyl heard the shots that answered the stunner, slug-throwers as well as powerguns, but the real measure of the response was the barely-audible clink of bottles shattering.

Then the gasoline bombs ignited and silhouetted the building from the south.

Tyl stood on the pedestrian way atop the levee, wondering when somebody would get around to taking a shot at him just because he *was* standing.

"Three and four," he ordered as the heavily-laden troops scrambled up the steps to join him. "Across the river, climb over the barges. Kekkonan, you lead 'em, set up a perimeter on the other side.

"And *wait!*" he added, though Kekkonan didn't look like the sort you had to tell that to.

The rest of the company was moving in a steady stream, lighted between the two fires of the trucks and the south front of the building they had abandoned.

"Take 'em across, take 'em across!" Tyl shouted as the Slammers plodded past. The non-coms would

take the words as an order, and the rest of the
troops would get the idea.

The first two squads squirmed as they waited,
their guns now aimed toward both pincers of the
mob. Fifty meters of the west frontage of the City
Offices were clear of the rioters who would otherwise have lapped around it. It wasn't a formal
stand-off; just the tense waiting of male dogs growl-
ing as they sidled toward each other, not quite
certain what the next seconds would bring.

The last man was Sergeant Major Scratchard,
falling a further step behind his troops with every
step he took.

"We're releasing the prisoners!" boomed the
array of loudspeakers on the building roof. Simultaneous words from a dozen locations echoed themselves by the amount of time that sound from the
mechanical diaphragms lagged behind the electronic pulses feeding them.

"Second Squad, withdraw," Tyl ordered. He
felt as if his load of gear had halved in weight
when the eyes of the rioters, orange flecks lighted
by the fires of their violence, turned away from
him and his men to stare at the City Offices.

Tyl jumped back down the steps and put his left
arm—the submachinegun was under his right arm-
pit—around the sergeant major's chest. Scratchard
weighed over a hundred kilos, only a little of it in
the gut that had expanded with his desk job. Tyl's
blood jumped with so much adrenalin that he
noticed only Scratchard's inertia—not his weight.

"Lemme go!" Scratchard rasped in a voice tight
with the ache in his knees.

"Shut the hell up!" Tyl snarled back. The laser
communicator was crushed between them, biting
both men's thighs. If he'd had a hand free, he'd

have thrown the cursed thing against the concrete
levee.

The mob's chanted, "Freedom!" gave way suddenly to a long bellow, loud and growing like a
peal of thunder. Tyl's back was to the City Offices,
and the rolling triumph had started on the far side
anyway, where the jail entrance opened onto the
parking area. He knew what was happening,
though.

And he knew, even before the shouts turned to
"*Kill* them! *Kill* them!" that this mob wasn't going
to be satisfied with freeing their fellows.

Likely the police trapped inside the building
had known that too; but they didn't have any
better choices either.

"You, give us a hand!" Tyl ordered as he and
Scratchard stumbled toward the railing across the
walkway. He pointed to the nearest trooper with
the gun that filled his right hand. She jumped to
her feet and took the sergeant major's other arm
while Tyl boomed over the radio, "First Squad,
withdraw. Kekkonan, make sure you've got us
covered."

The river here was half a kilometer wide between the levees, but with night sights and
powerguns, trained men could sweep the far walkway clear if some of the rioters decided it'd be safe
to pursue.

The river had fallen more than a meter since
Tyl viewed it six hours before. The barges still
floated a safe jump beneath the inner walkway of
the levee— but not safe for Jack Scratchard with a
load of gear.

"Gimme my arms free," the sergeant major
ordered.

Tyl nodded and stepped away with the trooper

on the other side. Scratchard gripped the railing
with both hands and swung himself over. He
crouched on the narrow lip, choosing his support,
and lowered himself onto the hogsheads with which
the barge was loaded. The troopers waiting to
help the senior non-com had the sense to get out
of the way.

"I'm fine now," Scratchard grunted. "Let's move!"

The barges were moored close, but there was
enough necessary slack in the lines that some of
them were over a meter apart while their rubber
bumpers squealed against those of the vessel on
the opposite flank. Tyl hadn't thought the problem through, but Kekkonan or one of the other
sergeants had stationed pairs of troopers at every
significant gap. They were ready to guide and
help lift later-comers over the danger.

"Thank the Lord," Tyl muttered as four strong
arms boosted him from the first barge to the next
in line. He wasn't sure whether he meant for the
help or for the realization that the men he commanded were as good as anybody could pray.

CHAPTER TWELVE

Charles Desoix wore a commo helmet to keep in touch with his unit, but he was looking out over Bamberg City with a hand-held image intensifier instead of using the integral optics of the helmet's face shield. The separate unit gave him better illumination, crisper details. He held the imager steady by resting his elbows on the rail of the porch outside the Consistory Room, overlooking the courtyard and beyond—

The railing jiggled as someone else leaned against it, bouncing Desoix's forty-magnification image of a window in the City Office building off his screen.

"*Lord* cur—" Desoix snarled as he spun. He wasn't the sort to slap the clumsy popinjay whom he assumed had disturbed him, but he was willing to give the contrary impression at the moment.

Anne McGill was at the rail beside him.

"They told me—" Desoix blurted.

99

"Yes, but I couldn't—" Anne said, both of them trying to cover the angry outburst that would disappear from reality if they pretended it hadn't occurred.

She'd closed the clear doors behind her, but Desoix could see into the Consistory Room. Enough light fell onto the porch to illuminate them for anyone looking in their direction.

He put his arms around Anne anyway, being careful not to gouge her back with a corner of the imaging unit. She didn't protest as he thought she might—but she gasped in surprise as her breasts flattened against her lover.

"Ah," Desoix said. "Yeah, I thought I'd wear my armor while I was out. . . . Ah, maybe we ought to go inside."

"No," Anne said, squeezing him tighter. "Just hold me."

Desoix stroked her back with his free hand while the breeze brought screams and the smell of smoke from across the river.

His helmet hissed with the sound of a Situation Report. He'd programmed Control to call for a sitrep every fifteen minutes during the night. That was the only way you could be sure an outlying unit hadn't been wiped out before they could sound an alarm. . . .

That wasn't a way Charles Desoix liked to think.

"Just a second, love," he muttered, blanking his mind of what the woman with her arms around him had started to say.

"Two to Control, all clear," a human voice said. "Over."

Gun Two was north of the city on a bluff overlooking the river. It had a magnificent field of fire—and there was very little development in the vicinity, which made it fairly safe in the present circumstances.

"Control to Three," said the emotionless artificial intelligence in the palace basement. "Report, over."

The hollow sound of gasoline bombs igniting, deadened by the pillow of intervening air, accompanied the gush of fresh orange flames from across the river. One side of the City Offices was covered with crawling fire.

"Three t' Control," came the voice of Sergeant Blaney.

There was a whining noise behind the words, barely audible through the commo link. It nagged at Desoix's consciousness, but he couldn't quite remember. . . .

"It's all right here," the human voice continued, "but there's a lot of traffic in and out of the plaza. There's fires north of us, and there's shots all round."

The sergeant paused. He wasn't speaking to Control but rather in the hope that Borodin or Desoix were listening even without an alert—and that they'd do something about the situation.

"Nothing aimed at us, s' far as we can tell," Blaney concluded. "Over."

The mechanical whining had stopped some seconds before.

Men, lighted by petroleum flares in both direction, were headed from the City Offices to the adjacent levee. Desoix couldn't make out who they were without the imaging unit, but he had a pretty good idea.

His left hand massaged Anne McGill's shoulders, to calm her and calm him as well. He reached for his helmet's commo key with his right hand, careful not to clash the two pieces of sophisticated hardware together, and said, "Blue to Three. Give me an azimuth on your gun, Blaney. Over."

Major Borodin was Red. With luck, he wasn't monitoring the channel just now.

Blaney hesitated, but he knew the XO could get the data from Control as easily—and that if Desoix asked, he already knew the answer even though Gun Three was far out of direct sight of the Palace of Government. "Sir," he said at last. "It's two-five-zero degrees. Over."

Normal rest position for Gun Three was 165^0, pointing out over Nevis Channel in the direction from which hostile ship-launched missiles were most likely to come. The crew had just re-aimed their weapon to cover the east stairs of the plaza. That was what *they* obviously thought was the most serious threat of their own well-being.

"Blue to Three," said Charles Desoix. "Over and out."

He wasn't down there with them, and he wasn't about to overrule their assessment of the situation from up here.

"Eunice is so angry," Anne McGill murmured. Communicating with the man beside her was as important to her state of mind as the strength of his arm around her shoulders. "I'm afraid, mostly—" and the simplicity of the statement belied its truth "—and so's John, I think, though it's hard to tell with him. But Eunice would like to hang them all, starting with the Bishop."

"Not going to be easy to do," Desoix said calmly while he adjusted the imager one-handed and prayed that it wouldn't show what he thought he saw in the shuddering flames.

It did. Men and women in police uniforms were

being thrown from the roof of the office building. They didn't fall far: just a meter or two, before they were halted jerking by the ropes around their necks.

Within the Consistory Room, voices burbled. Light brightened momentarily as someone turned up a wall sconce. It dimmed again as abruptly when common sense overcame a desire for gleaming surroundings.

The clear panels surrounding the circular room were shatterproof vitril. They were supposed to stop bricks or a slug from any weapon a man could fire from his shoulder, and the layer of gold foil within the thermoplastic might even deflect a powergun bolt.

But only a fool would insist on testing them while he was on the other side of the panel. That kind of test was a likely result of making the Consistory Room a beacon on a night like this.

Anne straightened slightly when she heard the sounds in the room behind them, but she didn't move away as Desoix had expected her to do. "There!" she said in a sharp whisper, pointing down toward the river. "They're moving . . . They—are they coming for us?"

Desoix used both hands to steady the imager, though he kept the magnification down to ten power. The fuel fires provided quite a lot of light, and the low clouds scattered it broadly for the intensification circuits.

"Those are Hammer's men," the UDB officer said as the scene glowed saffron in the imager's field of view.

The troopers crossing the river on the barges moored there were foreshortened by the angle and flattened into two dimensions by the imaging circuitry, but there were a lot of them. Enough to be the whole unit, the Lord willing—and better the Slammers have the problems than United Defense Batteries.

Desoix's helmet said in Control's calm voice, "Captain Koopman of Hammer's Regiment has been calling the officer of the day on the general frequency. The OOD has not replied. Now Captain Koopman is calling you. Do you wish—"

"Patch him through," Desoix ordered. Anne's startled expression reminded him that she would think he was speaking to her, but there wasn't time to clear that up now.

"—warn the guards not to shoot at us?" came the voice of the Slammers captain he'd met just that morning. "I can't raise the bastards and I *don't* want any trouble."

"Desoix to Slammers, over?" the UDB officer said.

"Roger Desoix, over," Koopman responded instantly. The relief in the infantry captain's voice was as obvious as the threat in the previous phrase: if anybody started shooting at him and his men, he was planning to finish the job and worry later about the results.

"Tyl, I'm headed down to the front entrance right now," Desoix said. "It's quiet on this side, so don't let some recruit get nervous at the wrong time."

He'd lowered the imager and was stroking Anne's back fiercely with his free hand, feeling the soft cloth bunch and ripple over skin still softer. Her arm was around his hips, beneath the rim of his armor, caressing him as well. Hard to believe this was the woman who'd always refused to lie down on a bed with him, because if her hair-do was mussed, people might guess what she'd been doing.

Desoix turned and kissed her, vaguely amazed that the tension of the moment increased his sexual arousal instead of dampening it.

"Love," he said, and *meant* "love," for the first time in a life during which he'd used the word to a hundred woman on a score of planets. "I'm going downstairs for a moment. I'll be back soon, but wait inside."

Even as he kissed her warm lips again, he was moving toward the door and carrying the woman with him by the force of his arm as well as by his personality.

Desoix felt a moment's concern as he strode for the elevator across the circular room that he'd left his mistress to be spiked by the wondering eyes of the dozen or more men who stood in nervous clumps amidst the furniture. Anne was going to have to handle that herself, because he couldn't take her with him into what he was maybe getting into—

And if he didn't go, well—he didn't need what he'd heard in Tyl Koopman's voice to know how a company of Hammer's Slammers was going to respond if a bunch of parade-ground soldiers tried to bar their escape from a dangerous situation.

CHAPTER THIRTEEN

The way some of the Executive Guards in the rotunda were waving their weapons around would have bothered Desoix less if he'd believed the men involved had ever fired their guns deliberately. A couple of them might honestly not know the difference between the trigger and the safety catch, making the polished-marble room as dangerous as a foxhole at the sharp end of the front.

If Koopman's unit blew off the flood shutters and tossed in grenades, the rotunda was going to be as dangerous as an abattoir.

Captain Rene Sanchez must have been off-duty by now, but there were more guards in the rotunda than the usual detachment and he was among them.

"Rene," Desoix called cheerfully as he stepped off the elevator, noticing that the Bamberg officer had unlatched the flap covering his pistol. "I've

107

come to give you a hand. We're getting some
reinforcements, Hammer's men. They're on the
way now."

Sanchez turned with a wild expression. "Nobody comes in or out," he said in a voice whose
high pitch increased the effect of his eyes being
focused somewhere close to infinity. The Guardsman was either drugged to a razor's edge, or his
nerves unaided had honed him to the same dangerous state.

"We're going to take care of this, Rene," Desoix
said, putting a friendly hand on Sanchez's shoulder.

The local man was quivering and it wasn't just
fear. Sanchez was ready to go, go off in *any* direction. He was in prime shape to lead a night assault
with knives and grenades—and he was just about
as lethal as a live grenade, too.

You could never tell about the ones who'd never
in their lives done anything real. They could react
any way at all when the universe forced itself to
their attention. About all a professional like Charles
Desoix knew to expect was that he wouldn't like
the result, whatever it turned out to be.

The Guard Commandant, Colonel Drescher, was
present. Arm in arm with Sanchez, the UDB officer walked toward him. Desoix had nodded to
Drescher in the past, but they had never spoken.

"Colonel," he said, using Rene Sanchez and a
brisk manner as his entree, "We've got some reinforcements coming in a few moments. I'm here to
escort them in."

"Charles, I got a squad in the courtyard now,"
said Desoix's helmet. "Let's get a door open, all
right? Over."

He didn't respond to Koopman's call, because
the Guards colonel was saying, "You? UDB? I'm

sorry, mister mercenary, the Marshal has given orders that the shutters not be opened."

"I just came from Marshal Dowell in the Consistory Room," Desoix said, letting his voice rise as only control had kept it from doing earlier. The best way to play this was to pretend to be on the edge of blind panic. That wasn't so great a pretense as he would have wished.

"He *ordered* me down here to inform you," Desoix continued. He thought he'd glimpsed Dowell upstairs. Certainly that was possible, at any rate. "By the Lord! man. Do you realize what the Marshal will do if you endanger him by keeping out his reinforcements? He'll have you—well, it's obvious."

The Guards colonel blinked. "Jorge Dowell doesn't give *me* orders!" he snapped, family pride overwhelming whatever trace of military obedience was in Drescher's make-up.

The Executive Guard was enough a law unto itself that Desoix had been sure that Drescher's references to army orders was misdirection—though Dowell might well have given such orders if anybody had bothered to ask him.

But because they hadn't . . . Desoix's present bluff wasn't beyond the realm of Dowell's possible response either.

"Still," Colonel Drescher continued. "Since you're here, we'll make an exception for courtesy's sake."

The waxen calm of his expression lapsed into gray fear for a moment. "But be quick, Lieutenant, or I swear I'll shut you out with them and the animals across the river."

Soldiers who'd been listening to the exchange touched the undogging mechanism without or-

ders, but they paused and drew back instead of
engaging the gears to slide the shutters away.

"Well get on with it!" cried another voice.

One of the guards pressed the switch before
Desoix's hand reached it; the UDB officer glanced
at the speaker instead.

There were four men together. They were wearing civilian clothes now in place of the ornate
uniforms they'd worn in the Consistory Room this
morning and in days past. The considerable entourage behind them stretched beyond the rotunda: servants, very few of them real bodyguards
—but most of the males were now armed with
rifles and pistols which looked as though they
came from government stores.

"Charles, how we holding?" came Tyl Koopman's
voice through the commo helmet. "Over."

The words lacked the overtone of threat that
had been in his earlier query. The Slammers could
see or at least hear that a door was opening.

"Blue to Slammers," Desoix responded. He could
feel a smile starting to twitch the corners of his
mouth. "Just a second. There's some restructuring
going on in here and we're, ah, making room for
you in the guest quarters. Let these folks pass."

Desoix made sure that he was with the quartet
of wealthy landholders as they forced their way
through the door ahead of their servants.

"No, no," one of the men was saying to another.
"My townhouse will have to take care of itself. I'm
off to my estates to rally support for the President.
I'll inform John of what I'm doing just as soon as I
get there, but of course I couldn't waste time *now*
with goodbyes."

Desoix thought for a moment that Captain Sanchez would step outside with him because that

was the direction in which the Guards officer had last been pointed. Sanchez was lost in the turmoil, though, and Desoix stood alone beside the door as minor rats streamed out past him, following the lead of the noble rats they served.

Fires glowed against the cloud cover from at least a dozen directions in the city, not just the vicinity of the City Offices directly across the river. The smell of burning was more noticeable here than it had been on the porch six meters high.

Desoix looked up. The porch was a narrow roof above him. He couldn't tell from this angle whether Anne McGill had stayed inside as he'd ordered, or if she were out in the night again watching for him, watching for hope.

"You, sir," a soldier said with enough emphasis to make the question a demand. "You our UDB liaison?"

"Roger," Desoix said. "I'm—"

But the close-coupled soldier in Slammers battle-dress was already relaying the information on his unit frequency.

There were several dozen of Hammer's men in the courtyard already. More were arriving with every passing moment. He didn't see Captain Koopman or the sergeant major he'd met once or twice before Tyl had arrived to take command.

The troopers jogged across the open street, hunched over. When they reached the courtyard they slowed. The veterans swept the Palace's empty, shuttered walls with their eyes, waiting for the motion that would unmask gunports and turn the paved area into a killing ground unless they shot first.

The new recruits only stared, more confused than frightened but certainly frightened enough.

"They know something we don't?" asked the Slammers non-com with KEKKONAN stenciled on his helmet. He nodded in the direction of the servants, the last of whom were clearing the doorway.

"They know they're scared," Desoix said.

Kekkonan laughed. "That just shows they're breathin'," he said.

He grunted something into his commo helmet— waved left-handed to Desoix because his right hand was on the grip of his slung submachinegun— and trotted into the rotunda with his troopers filing along after him.

The UDB officer had intended to lead the Slammers inside himself to avoid problems with the Bamberg guards. He hadn't moved quickly enough, but that wasn't likely to matter. Nobody with good sense was going to get in the way of *those* jacked-up killers.

Ornamental lighting still brightened the exterior of the palace, though the steel-shuttered facade looked out of place in a glittering myriad of tiny spotlights. It illuminated well the stooped forms in khaki and gray ceramic armor as they arrived, jogging because their loads were too heavy for them to run faster.

There were six in the last group, four troopers carrying a fifth while Captain Tyl Koopman trotted along behind with a double load of guns and bandoliers.

Casualty, Desoix thought, but Sergeant Major Scratchard was cursing too fluently for anyone to think his wound was serious.

"Listen, you idiots," Scratchard said in a voice of sudden calm as the UDB officer ran up to help.

"If you don't let me down now we're under the lights, I got no authority from here on out. Your choice, Cap'n."

"Right, we'll all walk from here," said Koopman easily. He handed one of the guns he carried to Scratchard while looking at Desoix. "Lieutenant," he added, "I'm about as glad to see you as I remember being."

Desoix looked over the other officer's shoulder toward the fires and shouts across the river. For a moment he thought it was his imagination that the sounds were coming closer.

Light flickering through the panels of the mall disabused him of his hopes. A torch-lit column was marching over the river. What the rioters had done to the City Offices suggested that they weren't headed for the cathedral now to pray for peace.

"Let's get inside," said Charles Desoix. "When this is all over, then you can thank me."

He didn't need to state the proviso: *assuming either of us is still alive.*

CHAPTER FOURTEEN

Tyl hadn't ridden in the little elevator off the back of the rotunda before. He and the UDB officer just about filled it, and neither of them was a big man.

Of course, in his armor and equipment Tyl wasn't the slim figure he would have cut in coveralls alone.

"Don't like to leave the guys before we know just what's happening here," he said aloud, though he was speaking as much to his own conscience as to the UDB officer beside him.

Tyl would have hated to be bolted behind steel shutters below, where the sergeant major was arranging temporary billets for the troops. The windowed Consistory Room was the next best thing to being outside—

And headed *away* from this Lord-stricken place!

"Up here is where we learn what's happening,"

115

Desoix said reasonably, nodding toward the elevator's ceiling. "Or at least as much as anyone in the government knows," he added with a frown which echoed the doubt in his words.

The car stopped with only a faint burring from its magnetic drivers. The doors opened with less sound even than that. Tyl strode into the Consistory Room.

He was Colonel Hammer's representative and the ranking Slammer on this continent. So long as he remembered that, nobody else was likely to forget.

There were fewer people in the big room than there had been in the morning, but their degree of agitation made the numbers seem greater. Marshal Dowell was present with a pair of aides, but those three and the pair of mercenaries were the only men in uniform.

The Chastain brothers smiled with frozen enthusiasm when Tyl nodded to them. They wore dark suits of conservative cut—and of natural offplanet fabrics that gave them roughly the value of an air car. Everyone else in the room was avoiding the Chastains. Backs turned whenever one of the twins attempted to make eye contact.

Berne, the City Prefect, didn't have even a twin for company. He huddled in the middle of the room like a clothes-pole draped with the green velour of his state robe.

"Where are—" Tyl began, but he'd already lost his companion. Lieutenant Desoix was walking briskly toward the large-framed woman who seemed to be an aide to the President's wife. Neither the President nor Eunice Delcorio were here at—

Servants opened the door adjacent to the elevator. John Delcorio entered a step ahead of his wife, but only because of the narrowness of the portal. Eunice was again in a flame-red dress. This one was demure in the front but cut with no back at all and a skirt that stretched to allow her legs to scissor back and forth as she moved.

Tyl hadn't found a sexual arrangement satisfactory to him on the freighter that brought him to Bamberia, and there'd been no time to take care of personal business since he touched down. He felt a rush of lust. It was a little disconcerting under the circumstances—

But on the other hand, it was nice to be reminded that there was more to life than the sorts of things that'd been going on in the past few hours.

"You there!" President Delcorio said unexpectedly. He glared at Tyl, his black eyes glowing like coal in a coking furnace. "Do you have to wear *that?*"

Tyl glanced down at where Delcorio pointed with two stubby, sturdy fingers together.

"This?" said the Slammers officer. His submachinegun hung from his right shoulder in a patrol sling that held it muzzle forward and grip down at his waist. He could seize it by reflex and spray whatever was in front of him without having to aim or think.

"Yessir," he explained. He spoke without concern, because it didn't occur to him that anyone might think he was offering insolence instead of information. "Example for the troops, you know. I told 'em nobody moved without a gun and bandolier —sleeping, eating, whatever."

Tyl blinked and looked back at the President. "Besides," he added. "I *might* need it, the way things are."

Delcorio flushed. Tyl realized that he and the President were on intersecting planes. Though the two of them existed in the same universe, almost none of their frames of reference were identical.

That was too bad. But it wasn't a reason for Tyl Koopman to change; not now, when it was pretty curst obvious that the instincts he'd developed in Hammer's Slammers were the ones most applicable here.

Eunice Delcorio laughed, a clear, clean sound that cut like a knife. "At least there's somebody who understands the situation," she said, echoing Tyl's thought and earning the Slammers officer another furious glance by her husband.

"I think we can all agree that the situation won't be improved by silly panic," Delcorio said mildly as his eyes swept the room. "Dowell, what do you have to report?"

There had been movement all around the room with the arrival of the Delcorios' but it was mostly limited to heads turning. Major Borodin, who'd been present after all—standing so quietly by a wall that Tyl's quick survey had missed him—was marching determinedly toward his executive officer. Desoix himself was alone. His lady-friend had left him at once to join her mistress, the President's wife.

But at the moment, everyone's attention was on Marshal Dowell, because that was where the President was looking.

"Yes, well," the army chief said. "I've given orders that a brigade be returned from Two as quickly as possible. You must realize that it's necessary for the troops to land as a unit so that their effect won't be dissipated."

"What about *now?*" cried the City Prefect. He stepped forward in an access of grief and rage, fluttering his gorgeous robes like a peacock preparing to fly. "You said you'd support my police, but your precious soldiers did *nothing* when those scum attacked the City Offices!"

One of Dowell's aides was speaking rapidly into a communicator with a shield that made the discussion inaudible to the rest of the gathering. The marshal glanced at him, then said, "We're still not sure what the situation over there is, and at any rate—"

"They took the place," Tyl said bluntly.

In the Slammers you didn't stand on ceremony when your superiors had bad data or none at all in matters that could mean the life of a lot of people. "Freed their friends, set fire to the building—hung at least some of the folks they caught. Via, you can see it from here, from the window."

He gestured with an elbow, because to point with his full arm would have moved his hand further from the grip of his weapon than instinct wanted to keep it at present.

Perhaps because everyone followed the gesture toward the panels overlooking the courtyard, the chanted . . . *freedom* . . . echoing from that direction became suddenly audible in the Consistory Room.

Across the room, the concealed elevator suctioned and snapped heads around. The officer Desoix had nodded to downstairs, the CO of the Executive Guard, stepped out with a mixture of arrogance and fear. He moved like a rabbit loaded with amphetamines. "Gentlemen!" he called in a clear voice. "Rioters are in the courtyard with guns and torches!"

Tyl was waiting for a recommendation—*do I have your permission to open fire?* was how a Slammers officer would have proceeded—but this fellow had nothing in mind save the theatrical announcement.

What Tyl didn't expect—nobody expected—was for Eunice Delcorio to sweep like a torch flame to the door and step out onto the porch.

The blast of noise when the clear doors opened was a shocking reminder of how well they blocked sound. There was an animal undertone, but the organized chant of *"Freedom!"* boomed over and through the snarl until the mob recognized the black-haired, glass-smooth woman facing them from the high porch.

Tyl moved fast. He was at Eunice's side before the shouts of surprise had given way to the hush of a thousand people drawing breath simultaneously. He thought there might be shots. At the first bang or spurt of light he was going to hurl Eunice back into the Consistory Room, trusting his luck and his clamshell armor.

Not because she was a woman; but because if the President's wife got blown away, there was as little chance of compromise as there seemed to be of winning until the brigade from Two arrived.

And maybe a little because she was a woman.

"What will you have, citizens?" Eunice called.

The porch was designed for speeches. Even without amplification, the modeling walls threw her powerful contralto out over the crowd. "Will you abandon God's Crusade for a whim?"

The uplifted faces were a blur to Tyl in the scatter of light sources that the mob carried. The crosses embroidered in white cloth on the left shoulders of their garments were clear enough to be recognized, though—and that was true whether the base color was red or black.

There was motion behind him, but Tyl had eyes only for the mob.

Weapons glinted there. He couldn't tell if any of them were being aimed. The night-vision sensors in his faceshield would have helped; but if he locked the shield down he'd be a mirror-faced threat to the crowd, and that might be all it took to draw the first shots. . . .

Desoix'd stepped onto the porch. He stood on the other side of Eunice Delcorio, and he was cursing with the fluency of a mercenary who's sleep-learned a lot of languages over the years.

The other woman was on the porch too. From the way the UDB officer was acting, she'd preceded rather than followed him.

The crowd's silence had dissolved in a dozen varied answers to Eunice's question, all underlain by blurred attempts to continue the chant of "Freedom!"

Something popped from the center of the mob. Tyl's left arm reached across Eunice's waist and was a heartbeat short of hurling the woman back through the doors no matter who stood behind her. A white flare burst fifty meters above the courtyard, harmless and high enough that it could be seen by even the tail of the mob stretching across the river.

The mob quieted after an anticipatory growl that shook the panels of the doors.

There was a motion at the flagstaff, near where the flare had been launched. Before Tyl could be sure what was happening, a hand-held floodlight glared over the porch from the same location.

He stepped in front of the President's wife,

bumping her out of the way with his hip, while his
left hand locked the faceshield down against the
blinding radiance. The muzzle of his submachinegun
quested like an adder's tongue while his finger
took up slack on the trigger.

"Wait!" boomed a voice from the mob in amplified startlement. The floodlight dimmed from a
threat to comfortable illumination.

"I'll take over now, Eunice," said John Delcorio
as his firm hand touched Tyl's upper arm, just
beneath the shoulder flare of the clamshell armor.

The Slammers officer stepped aside, knowing it
was out of his hands for better or for worse, now.

President Delcorio's voice thundered to the
crowd from roof speakers, "My people, why do
you come here to disturb God's purpose?"

Through his shield's optics, Tyl could see that
there were half a dozen priests in dark vestments
grouped beside the flagpole. They had a guard of
orderlies from the House of Grace, but both the
man with the light and the one raising a bull-horn
had been ordained. Tyl thought, though the distance made uncertain, that the priest half-hidden
behind the pole was Father Laughlin.

None of the priests carried weapons. All the
twenty or so orderlies of their bodyguard held guns.

"We want the murderer Berne!" called the bull
horn. The words were indistinct from the out-of-
synchronous echoes which they waked from the
Palace walls. "Berne sells justice and sells lives!"

"Berne!" shouted the mob, and their echoes
thundered BERNE*berne*berne.

As the echoes died away, Tyl heard Desoix
saying in a voice much louder than he intended,
"Anne, for the *Lord's* sake! Get back inside!"

"Will you go back to your homes in peace if I

replace the City Prefect?" Delcorio said, pitching his words to make his offered capitulation sound like a demand. His features were regally arrogant as Tyl watched him sidelong behind the mirror of his faceshield.

The priest with the bull-horn leaned sideways to confer with the bigger man behind the flagpole, certainly Father Laughlin. While the mob waited for their leaders' response, the President used the pause to add, "One man's venality can't be permitted to jeopardize God's work!"

"Give us Berne!" demanded the courtyard.

"I'll replace—" Delcorio attempted.

GIVE*give*give roared the mob. GIVE*give*give. . . .

Eunice leaned over to say something to her husband. He held up a hand to silence the crowd. The savage voices boomed louder, a thousand of them in the courtyard and myriads more filling the streets beyond.

A woman waved a doll in green robes above her head. She held it tethered by its neck.

Delcorio and his wife stepped back into the Consistory Room. Their hands were clasped so that it was impossible to tell who was leading the other. The President reached to slide the door shut for silence, but Lieutenant Desoix was close behind with an arm locked around the other woman's waist. His shoulder blocked Delcorio's intent.

Tyl Koopman wasn't going to be the only target on the balcony while the mob waited for a response it might not care for. He kept his featureless face to the front—with the gun muzzle beneath it for emphasis—as he retreated after the rest.

CHAPTER FIFTEEN

"Firing me won't—" Berne began even before Tyl slid the door shut on the thunder of the mob.

"I'm not sure we can defend—" Marshal Dowell was saying with a frown and enough emphasis that he managed to be heard.

"Be silent!" Eunice Delcorio ordered in a glass-sharp voice.

The wall thundered with the low notes of the shouting in the courtyard.

Everyone in the Consistory Room had gathered in a semi-circle. They were facing the porch and those who had been standing on it.

There were only a dozen or so of Delcorio's advisors present. Twice that number had awaited when Tyl followed Eunice out to confront the mob, but they were gone now.

Gone from the room, gone from the Palace if

they could arrange it—and assuredly gone from
the list of President Delcorio's supporters.

That bothered Tyl less than the look of those
who remained. They glared at the City Prefect
with the expression of gorgeously-attired fish view-
ing an injured one of their number . . . an equal
moments before, a certain victim now. The eyes
of Dowell's aides were hungry as they slid over
Berne.

Eunice Delcorio's voice had carved a moment
of silence from the atmosphere of the Consistory
Room. The colonel of the Executive Guard filled
the pause with, "It's quite *im*possible to defend
the Palace from numbers like that. We can't even
think of— "

"Yeah, we could hold it," Tyl broke in.

He'd forgotten his faceshield was locked down
until he saw everyone start away from him as if he
were something slime-covered that had just crawled
through a window. With the shield in place, the
loudspeaker built into his helmet cut in automatically—so they *weren't* going to ignore him if he
raised his voice.

He didn't want to be ignored, but he flipped up
the shield to be less threatening now that he had
the group's attention.

"You've got what, two companies?" he went on,
waving his left index finger toward the glittering
colonel. All right, they weren't the Slammers; but
they had assault rifles and they weren't exactly
facing combat infantry either.

"We've got a hundred men," he said. "*Curst*
good ones, and the troops the UDB's got here in
the Palace know how to handle— "

Tyl had nodded in the direction of Lieutenant

Desoix, but it was Borodin, the battery commander, who interrupted, "I have no men in the Palace."

"Huh?" said the Slammers officer.

"What?" Desoix said. "We have the off-duty c—"

"I'm worried about relieving the crews with the, ah—" Borodin began.

He looked over at the President. The mercenary commander couldn't whisper the explanation, not now. "The conditions in the streets are such that I wasn't sure we'd be able to relieve the gun crews normally, so I ordered the reserve crews to billet at the guns so that we could be sure that there'd be a full watch alert if the enemy tries to take advantage of . . . events."

"*Events!*" snarled John Delcorio.

The door behind him rattled sharply when a missile struck it. The vitril held as it was supposed to do.

"John, they aren't after *me*," Berne cried with more than personal concern in his voice. He was right, after all, everybody else here must know that, since it was so obvious to Tyl Koopman in his first day on-planet. "You mustn't—"

"If you hadn't failed, none of this would be happening," Eunice said, her scorn honed by years of personal hatred that found its outlet now in the midst of general catastrophe.

She turned to her husband, the ends of her black hair emphasizing the motion. "Why are you delaying? They want this criminal, and that will give us the time we need to deal with the filth properly with the additional troops."

Vividness made Eunice Delcorio a beautiful woman, but the way her lips rolled over the word "properly" sent a chill down the spine of everyone who watched her.

Berne made a break for the door to the hall.

Tyl's mind had been planning the defense of the Palace of Government. Squads of the local troops in each wing to fire as soon as rioters pried or blasted off a flood shutter to gain entrance. Platoons of mercenaries poised to react as fire brigades, responding to each assault with enough violence to smother it in the bodies of those who'd made the attempt. Grenadiers on the roof; they'd very quickly clear the immediate area of the Palace of everything except bodies and the moaning wounded.

Easy enough, but they were answers to questions that nobody was asking any more. Besides, they could only hold the place for a few days against tens of thousands of besiegers—only long enough for the brigade to arrive from Two, if it came.

And Tyl was a lot less confident of that point than the President's wife seemed to be.

A middle-aged civilian tripped the City Prefect. One of Dowell's aides leaped on Berne and wrestled him to the polished floor as he tried to rise, while the other aide shouted into his communicator for support without bothering to lock his privacy screen in place.

Tyl looked away in disgust. He caught Lieutenant Desoix's eye. The UDB officer wore a bland expression.

But he wasn't watching the scuffle and the weeping prefect either.

"All right," said the President, bobbing his head in decision. "I'll tell them."

He took one stride, reached for the sliding door,

and paused. "You," he said to Tyl. "Come with me."

Tyl nodded without expression. Another stone or possibly a light bullet whacked against the vitril. He set his faceshield and stepped onto the porch ahead of the Regiment's employer.

He didn't feel much just now, though he wanted to take a piss real bad. Even so, he figured he'd be more comfortable facing the mob than he was over what had just happened in the Consistory Room.

The crowd roared. Behind his shield, Tyl grinned —if that was the right word for the way instinct drew up the corners of his mouth to bare his teeth. There was motion among the up-turned faces gleaming like the sputum the sea leaves when it draws back from the strand.

Something pinged on the railing. Tyl's gun quivered, pointed—

"Wait!" thundered the bull-horn.

"My people!" boomed the President's voice from the roofline. He rested his palms wide apart on the railing.

He'd followed after all, a step behind the Slammers officer just in case a sniper was waiting for the first motion. Delcorio wasn't a brave man, not as a professional soldier came to appraise courage, but his spirit had a tumbling intensity that made him capable of almost anything.

At a given moment.

The mob was making a great deal of disconnected noise. Delcorio trusted his amplified voice to carry him through as he continued, "I have dismissed the miscreant Berne as you demanded. I will turn him over to the custody of the Church for safekeeping until the entire State can determine the punishment for his many crimes."

"Give us Berne!" snarled the bull-horn with echoing violence. It spoke in the voice of a priest but not a Christian; and the mob that took up the chant was not even human.

Delcorio turned and tried to shout something into the building with his unaided voice. Tyl couldn't hear him.

The President raised a hand for silence from the crowd. The chant continued unabated, but Delcorio and the Slammers officer were able to back inside without a rain of missiles to mark their retreat.

There was a squad of the Executive Guard in the Consistory Room. Four of the ten men were gripping the City Prefect. Several had dropped their rifles in the scuffle and no one had thought to pick the weapons up again.

Delcorio made a dismissing gesture. "Send him out to them," he said. "I've done all I can. Quickly, so I don't have to go out there—"

His face turned in the direction of his thoughts, toward the porch and the mob beneath. The flush faded and he began to shiver uncontrollably. Reaction and memory had caught up with the President.

There were only four civilian advisors in the room besides Berne. Five. A man whose suit was russet or gold, depending on the direction of the light, had been caught just short of getting into the elevator by Delcorio's return.

The Guards colonel was shaking his head. "No, no," he said. "That won't do. If we open a shutter, they'll be in and well, the way the fools are worked up, who knows what might happen?"

"But—" the President said, his jaw dropping.

He'd aged a decade since he stepped off the porch. Hormonal courage abandoned him to reaction and remembrance. "But I *must*. But I promised them, Drescher, and if I don't—"

His voice would probably have broken off there anyway, but a bellow from the courtyard in thunderous synchrony smothered all sound within for a moment.

"Pick him up, then, " said Eunice Delcorio in a voice as clear as a sapphire laser. "You four—*pick* him up and follow. We'll *give* them their scrap of bone."

She strode toward the door, the motion of her legs a devouring flame across the intaglio.

Berne screamed as the soldiers lifted him. Because he was screaming, no one heard Tyl Koopman say in a choked voice, "Lady, you *can't*—"

But of course they could. And Tyl had done the same or worse, checking out suspicious movements with gunfire, knowing full well that nine chances in ten, the victims were going to be civilians trying to get back home half an hour after curfew. . . .

He'd never have spent one of his own men this way; and he'd never serve under an officer who did.

Colonel Drescher threw open the door himself, though he stood back from the opening with a care that was more than getting out of the way of the President's wife.

Tyl stepped out beside her, because he'd made it his job . . . or Hammer had made it his job . . . and who in blazes cared, he was there and the animal snarl of the mob brought answering rage to the Slammer's mind and washed some of the sour taste from his mouth.

The Guardsmen in azure uniforms and Berne in green made a contrast as brilliant as a parrot's plumage as they manhandled the prefect to the railing under the glare of lights. Floods were trained from at least three locations in the courtyard now, turned high; but that was all right, they needed to watch this, sure they did.

Eunice cried something inaudible but imperious. She gestured out over the railing. The soldiers looked at one another.

Berne was screaming wordlessly. His eyes were closed, but tears poured from beneath the lids. He had fouled himself in his panic. The smell added the only element necessary to make the porch a microcosm of Hell.

Eunice gestured again. The Guards threw their prisoner toward the courtyard.

Berne grabbed the railing with both hands as he went over. His legs flailed without the organization needed to boost him back onto the porch, but his hands clung like claws of cast bronze.

Eunice gave a furious order that was no more than a grimace and a quick motion of her lips. Two of the soldiers tried gingerly to push Berne away. The prefect twisted his head and bit the hands of one. His eyes were open now and as mad as those of a back-ward psychotic. Bottles and stones began to fly from the crowd, clashing on the rail and floor of the porch.

The Guardsmen drew back into a huddle in the doorway. The man who still carried his rifle raised it one-handed to shield his face.

A bottle shattered on Tyl's breastplate. He didn't hear the shot that was fired a moment later, but the howl of a light slug ricocheting from the wall cut through even the roar of the crowd.

"*Get* inside!" Tyl's speakers bellowed to Eunice Delcorio as he stepped sideways to the railing where Berne thrashed. Tyl hammered the man's knuckles with the butt of his submachinegun. One stroke, two—bone cracked—

Three and the prefect's screaming changed note. His broken left hand slipped and his right hand opened. Berne's throat made a sound like a siren as he fell ten meters to the mob waiting to receive him.

Tyl turned. If the Guardsmen had still been blocking the doorway, he might have shot them . . . but they'd fled inside and Eunice Delcorio was sweeping after them. Her head was regally high, and she was ignoring the streak of blood over one cheekbone where a stone had cut her.

Tyl turned for a last look into the courtyard. The rioters were passing Berne hand to hand, over their heads, like a bit of green algae seen sliding through the gut of a paramecium. There was greater motion also; the mob was shifting back—only a compression in the crowd at the moment, but soon to turn into real movement that would clear the courtyard.

They were leaving, now that they had their bone.

As the City Prefect was passed along, those nearest were ripping bits away. For the moment, the bits were mostly clothing.

Tyl stepped into the Consistory Room and slammed the door behind him hard enough to shatter a panel that hadn't been armored. He left his faceshield down, because if none of them could see his expression, he could pretend that he wasn't really here.

"Lieutenant Desoix," said Major Borodin. He

wasn't speaking loudly, but no one else in the room was speaking at all. "Gun Three needs to be withdrawn. Will you handle that at once."

The battery commander's face looked like a mirror of what Tyl thought was on his own features.

"Nobody's withdrawing," said President Delcorio. He had his color back, and he stroked his hands together briskly as if to warm them. His eyes shifted like a sparkling fire and lighted on the Guards colonel. The hands stopped.

"Colonel Drescher," Delcorio said crisply. "I want your men on combat footing at once. Don't you have some other sort of uniforms? Like those."

One spade-broad hand gestured toward Tyl in khaki and armor. "Something suitable. This isn't a *parade*. We're at war. War."

"Well, I—" Drescher began. Everyone in the room was in a state of shock, hammered by events into a state that made them ready to be pressed in any direction by a strong personality.

For a moment, until the next stimulus came along.

"Well, get on with it!" the President snapped. While the squad of gay uniforms was just shifting toward the hall door, Delcorio's attention had already flashed across the other faces in the Consistory Room.

And found very few.

"Where's—" Delcorio began. "Where's—" His voice rose, driven by an emotion that was either fury or panic—and perhaps had not yet decided which it would be.

"Sir," said one of the Chastains, stepping forward to take the President by the hand. "Thom and I will—"

"*You!*" Delcorio screamed. "What are *you* doing here?"

"Sir," said Thom Chastain with the same hopeful-puppy expression as his brother. "We know you'll weather this—"

"You're spying, aren't you?" Delcorio cried, slapping at the offered hands as if they were beasts about to bite him. "Get *out*, don't you think I know it!"

"Sir—" said the two together in blank amazement.

The President's nephew Pedro stepped between the Chastain's and Delcorio. "Go on!" he snarled, looking like a bulldog barking at a pair of gangling storks. "We don't need you here. Get *out*!"

"But—" Richie Chastain attempted helplessly. Pedro, as broadly-built as his uncle, shoved the other men toward the door.

They fled in a swirl of robes and words whimpered to one another or to fate.

"You there," the President continued briskly. "Dowell. You'll have the additional troops in place by noon tomorrow. Do you understand? I don't care if they have to loot shops for their meals, they'll *be* here."

Delcorio spoke with an alert dynamism. It was hard to imagine that the same man had been on the edge of violent madness a moment before, and in a funk brief minutes still earlier.

Dowell saluted with a puzzled expression. He mumbled something to his aides. The three of them marched out the hall door without looking backward.

If they caught the President's eye again, he might hold them.

"And *you*, Major Borodin, you aren't going to

strip our city of its protection against the Christ-deniers," Delcorio said as he focused back on the battery commander.

The President should have forgotten the business of moving the gun—so much had gone on in the moments since. He hadn't forgotten, though. There *was* a mind inside that skull, not just a furnace of emotions.

If John Delcorio were as stupid as he was erratic, Tyl might have been able to figure out what in the Lord's name he ought best to be doing.

"*Do* you understand?" Delcorio insisted, pointing at the battery commander with two blunt fingers in a gesture as threatening as anything short of a gun muzzle could be.

"Yes sir," replied Major Borodin, his voice as stiff as the brace in which he held his body. "But I must tell you that I'm obeying under protest, and when I contact my superiors—"

"You needn't tell me anything, mercenary," the President interrupted without even anger to leaven the contempt in his words. "You need only do your job and collect your pay—which I assure you, your superiors show no hesitation in doing either."

"John," said Eunice Delcorio with a shrug that dismissed everything that was going on around her at the moment. "I'm going to call my brother again. They said they couldn't raise him when I tried earlier."

"Yes, I'll talk to him myself," the President agreed, falling in step beside the short woman as he headed toward the door to their private apartments. "He'd have nothing but a ten-hectare sharecrop if it weren't for me. If he thinks he can duck his responsibilities now. . . ."

"Anne," Desoix said in a low voice as Eunice's aide hesitated. She looked from her mistress to the UDB officer—and stayed

Pedro Delcorio raised an eyebrow, then nodded to the others as he followed his uncle out of the Consistory Room. There were only four of them left: the three mercenaries and Desoix's lady-friend.

The four of them, and the smell of fear.

CHAPTER SIXTEEN

"Let's get out of here," Koopman said.

Charles Desoix's heart leaped in agreement—then bobbed back to normalcy when he realized that the Slammers officer meant only to get out of the Consistory Room, onto the porch where the air held fewer memories of the immediate past.

Sure, Koopman was the stolid sort who probably didn't realize how badly things were going . . . and Charles Desoix wasn't going to support a mutiny, wasn't going to desert his employers because of trouble that hadn't—if you wanted to be objective about it—directly threatened the United Defense Batteries at all.

It was hard to be objective when you were surrounded by a mob of perhaps fifty thousand people, screaming for blood and quite literally tearing a man to pieces.

139

They were welcome to Berne—he was just as crooked as the bull-horn had claimed. But. . .

"What did you say, Charles?" Anne asked—which meant that Desoix had been speaking things that he shouldn't even have been thinking.

He hugged her reflexively. She jumped, also by reflex because she didn't try to draw further away when she thought about the situation. Major Borodin didn't appear to notice—or to care.

The courtyard was deserted, but the mob had left behind an amazing quantity of litter—bottles, boxes, and undefinable scraps; even a cloak, scarlet and apparently whole in the light of the wall sconces. It was as if Desoix were watching a beach just after the tide had ebbed.

Across the river, fires burned from at least a score of locations. Voices echoed, harsh as the occasional grunt of shots.

Like the tide, the mob would return.

"We've got to get out of here," Desoix mused aloud.

"She'll leave," Anne said with as much prayer in her voice as certainty. "If she stays, they'll do terrible things to. . . She *knows* that, she won't let it happen."

"Colonel wants me to hold if there's any chance to keep Delcorio in power," Koopman said to the night. There was a snicker of sound as he raised his faceshield, but he did not look at his companions as he spoke. "What's your bet on that, Charles?"

"Something between zip and zero," Desoix said. He was careful not to let his eyes fall on Anne or the major when he spoke; but it was no time to tell polite lies.

" 'bout what I figured too," the Slammers officer said mildly. He was leaning on his forearms while his fingers played with a dimple in the rail. After a moment, Desoix realized that the dimple had been hammered there by a bullet.

"I don't see any way we can abandon our positions in defiance of a direct order," Major Borodin said.

The battery commander set his fingers in his thinning hair and squeezed firmly, as though that would change the blank rotation of his thoughts. He took his hands away and added hurriedly to the Slammers officer, "Of course, that has nothing to do with you, Captain. My problem is that I have to defend the city, so I'm in default of the contract if I move my guns. Well, Gun Three. But that's the only one that seems to be in danger."

"Charles, you'll protect her if we leave, won't you?" asked Anne in sudden fierceness. She pulled on Desoix's shoulder until he turned to face her worries directly. "You won't let them have her to, to escape yourself, will you?"

He cupped her chin with his left hand. "Anne," he said. "If Eunice and the President just say the word, we'll have them safely out of here within the hour. Won't we, Tyl?" he added as he turned to the Slammers officer.

"Colonel says, maybe just a week or two," Koopman said unexpectedly. When his index finger burnished the bullet scar, the muzzle of his own slung weapon chinked lightly against the rail. "Suppose Delcorio could hold out a week?"

"Suppose we could hold out five minutes if they come back hard?" Desoix snapped, furious at the infantryman's response when finally it looked as if there were a chance to clear out properly. There wasn't any doubt that Eunice Delcorio could bend her husband to her own will. She was inflexible, with none of John Delcorio's flights and falterings.

If Anne worked on her mistress, it could all turn out reasonably. Exile for Delcorio on his huge private estates; safety for Anne McGill, whose mistress wasn't the only one with whom the mob would take its pleasure.

And release for the mercenaries who were at the moment trapped in this place by ridiculous orders.

"Yeah," said Koopman with a heavy sigh. He turned at last to face his companions. "Well, I'm not going to get any of my boys wasted for nothing at all. We aren't paid to be heroes. Guess I'll go down and tell Jack to pack up to move at daylight."

The Slammers officer quirked a grin to Desoix and nodded to Anne and the major as he stepped toward the door.

"Tyl, wait . . ." Desoix said as a word rang echoes. "Can you. . . Major, how many men do you have downstairs still?"

Borodin shrugged out of the brown study into which he had fallen as he watched the fires burning around him. "Men?" he repeated. "Senter and Lachere is all. We're still short—"

"Tyl, can you, ah—" Desoix went on. He paused, because he didn't want to use the wrong word, since what he was about to ask was no part of the Slammers' business.

"I need to get down to the warehouses on the corniche," Desoix said, rephrasing the question to make the request personal rather than military. "All I've got here are the battery clerks and they're not, ah, trained for this. Could you detail a few men, five or six, to go along with me in case there was a problem?"

"Lieutenant," Borodin said gruffly. "What do—"

"Sir," Desoix explained as the plan drew itself in glowing lines in his mind, the alternative sites and intersecting fields of fire. "When we get Gun Five set up, we can move Three a kilometer east on the corniche and still be in compliance. Five on the outskirts of town near Pestini's Chapel, Three on Guizer Head—and we've got everything Delcorio can demand under the contract."

"Without stationing any of our men down . . . ." Borodin said as the light dawned. He might have intended to point toward the plaza, but as his gaze turned out over the city, his voice trailed off instead.

Both UDB officers stared at Tyl Koopman.

Koopman shrugged. "I'll go talk to the guys," he said.

And they had to be satisfied with that, because he said nothing more as he walked back into the building.

CHAPTER SEVENTEEN

Tyl's functional company had taken over the end of a second-floor hallway abandoned by the entourage of six noble guests of the President. The hundred troopers had a great deal more room than there'd been in the City Office billet—or any normal billet.

And, though they'd lost their personal gear when the office building burned, the nobles' hasty departure meant that the soldiers could console themselves for the objects they'd lost across the river. Jewelry and rich fabrics peeked out the edges of khaki uniforms as Tyl strode past the corridor guard and into the billeting area.

Too bad about Aunt Sandra's jelly, though. He could turn over a lot of rich folks' closets and not find anything to replace that.

Troopers with makeshift bedrolls in the hallway were jumping to attention because somebody else had. The heads that popped from doorways were emptying the adjoining guest suites as effectively as if Tyl had shouted, "Fall in!"

Which was about the last thing he wanted.

"Settle down," he said with an angry wave of his arm, as if to brush away the commotion. They were all tight. The troops didn't know much, and that made them rightly nervous.

Tyl Koopman knew a good deal more, and what he'd seen from the porch wasn't the sort of knowledge to make anybody feel better about the situation.

"Captain?" said Jack Scratchard as he muscled his way into the hall.

Tyl motioned the sergeant major over. He keyed his commo helmet with the other hand and said loudly—most of the men didn't have their helmets on, and only the senior non-coms were fitted with implants—"At present, I'm expecting us to get the rest of the night's sleep here, but maybe not be around much after dawn. When I know more, you'll hear."

Scratchard joined him. The two men stepped out of the company area for the privacy they couldn't find within it. Tyl paused and called over his shoulder, "Use a little common sense in what you try to pack, all right?"

He glared at a corporal with at least a dozen vibrantly-colored dresses in her arms.

The remaining six suites off the hallway were as empty as those Scratchard had appropriated. He must have decided to keep the troops bunched up a little under the present circumstances, and Tyl wasn't about to argue with him.

The doors of all the suites had been forced. As they stepped into the nearest to talk, Tyl noticed that the richly-appointed room had been turned over with great care, although none of his soldiers were at present inside continuing their looting.

Loot and mud were the two constants of line service. If you couldn't get used to either one, you'd better find a rear-echelon slot somewhere.

"Talk to the Old Man?" Scratchard muttered when he was sure they were alone in the tumbled wreckage.

Tyl shrugged. "Not yet," he said. "Sent an all-clear through open channels, is all. It's mostly where we left it earlier, and I don't want Central—" he wasn't comfortable saying "Hammer" or even "the Old Man" "—thinking they got to wet-nurse me."

He paused, and only then got to the real business. "Desoix—the UDB Number Two," he said. "He wants a few guys to cover his back while he gets a calliope outa storage down to the seafront. Got everybody but a couple clerks out with the other tubes."

The sergeant major knuckled his scalp, the ridge where his helmet rode. "What's that do for us, the other calliope?" he asked.

"Bloody zip," Tyl answered with a shrug. *He* was in charge, but this was the sort of thing that the sergeant major had to be brought into.

Besides, nothing he'd heard about Ripper Jack Scratchard suggested that there'd be an argument on how to proceed.

"What it does," Tyl amplified, "is let them withdraw the gun they got down by the plaza. Desoix doesn't like having a crew down there, the way things're going."

Scartchard frowned. "Why can't he—" he began.

"Don't ask," Tyl said with a grimace.

The question made him think of things he'd rather forget. He thumbed in what might have been the direction of the Consistory Room and said, "It got real strange up there. Real strange."

He shook his head to rid it of the memories and added, "You know, he's the one I finally raised to get us into here before it really dropped in the pot. None of the locals were going to do squat for us."

"Doing favors is a good way t' get your ass blown away," Scratchard replied, sourly but without real emphasis. "But sure, I'll look up five guys that'd like t' see the outside again."

He grinned around the clothing strewn about them from forced clothes presses. "Don't guess it'll be too hard to look like civilians, neither."

"Ah," said Tyl. He was facing a blank wall. "Thought I might go along, lead 'em, you know."

"Like hell," said the sergeant major with a grin that seemed to double the width of his grizzled face. "*I* might, except for my knees. You're going to stay bloody here, in charge like you're supposed t' be."

His lips pursed. "Kekkonan 'll take 'em. He won't buy into anything he can't buy out of."

Tyl clapped the non-com on the shoulder. "Round 'em up," he said as he stepped into the hall. "I'll tell Desoix. This is the sort of thing that should've been done, you know, last week."

As he walked down the hall, the Slammers officer keyed his helmet to learn where Desoix was at the moment. Putting this sort of information on open channels didn't seem like a great idea, unless you had a lot more confidence in the Bamberg army than Tyl Koopman did.

Asking for volunteers in a business like this was

a waste of time. They were veteran troops, these; men and women who would parrot "never volunteer" the way they'd been told by a thousand generations of previous veterans . . . but who knew in their hearts that it was boredom that killed.

You couldn't live in barracks, looking at the same faces every waking minute, without wanting to empty a gun into one of them just to make a change.

So the first five soldiers Scratchard asked would belt on their battle gear with enthusiasm, bitching all the time about "When's it somebody else's turn to take the tough one?" They didn't want to die, but they didn't think they would . . . and just maybe they would have gone anyway, whatever they thought the risk was, because it was too easy to imagine the ways a fort like the Palace of Government could became a killing bottle.

They were Hammer's Slammers. They'd done that to plenty others over the years.

Tyl didn't have any concern that he'd be able to hand Desoix his bodyguards, primed and ready for whatever the fire-shot night offered.

And he knew that he'd give three grades in rank to be able to go along with them himself.

CHAPTER EIGHTEEN

The porch off the Consistory Room didn't have a view of anything Tyl wanted to see—the littered courtyard and, across the river, the shell of the City Offices whose windows were still outlined by the sullen glow in its interior. The porch was as close as he could come to being outside, though, and that was sufficient recommendation at the moment.

The top of the House of Grace was barely visible above the south wing of the Palace. The ghost of firelight from the office building painted the eyes and halo of the sculptured Bishop Trimer also.

Tyl didn't want company, so when the door slid open behind him, he turned his whole body. That way his slung submachinegun pointed, an "accident" that he knew would frighten away anyone except his own troopers—whom he could order to leave him alone.

151

Lieutenant Desoix's woman stopped with a little gasp in her throat, but she didn't back away.

"Via!" Tyl said in embarrassment, lifting the gun muzzle high and cursing himself in his head for the dumb idea. One of those dandies, he'd figured, or a smirking servant . . . except that the President's well-dressed advisors seemed to have pretty well disappeared, and the flunkies also.

Servants were getting thin on the ground, too.

"If you'd like to be alone . . . ?" the woman said, either polite or real perceptive.

"Naw, you're fine," Tyl said, feeling clumsy and a lot the same way as he had a few months ago. Then he'd been to visit a girl he might have married if he hadn't gone off for a soldier the way he had. "You're, ah—Lady Eunice's friend, aren't you?"

"That too," said the woman drily. She took the place Tyl offered at the railing and added, "My name's Anne McGill. And I believe you're Captain Koopman?"

"Tyl," the soldier said. "Rank's not for—" He gestured. "Out here."

She didn't look as big as she had inside. Maybe because he had his armor on now that he was standing close to her.

Maybe because he'd recently watched five big men put looted cloaks on over their guns and armor to go off with Lieutenant Desoix.

"Have you known Charles long?" she asked, calling Tyl back from a stray thought that had the woman wriggling out of her dark blue dress and offering herself to him.

He shook his head abruptly to clear the thought. Not his type, and he *sure* wasn't hers.

"No," he said, forgetting that she thought he'd

answered with the shake of his head. "I just got in today, you see. I don't recall we ever served with the UDB before. Anyhow, mostly you don't see much of anybody's people but your own guys."

It wasn't even so much that he was horny. Screwing was just something he could really lose himself in.

Killing was that way too.

"It's dangerous out there, isn't it?" she said. She wasn't looking at the city because her face was lifted too high. From the way her capable hands washed one another, she might well have been praying.

"Out there?" Tyl repeated bitterly. "Via, it's dangerous *here*, and we can't anything but bloody twiddle our thumbs."

Anne winced, as much at the violence as the words themselves.

Instantly contrite, Tyl said, "But you know, if things stay cool a little longer—no spark, you know, setting things off. . . . It may all work out."

He was repeating what Colonel Hammer had told him a few minutes before, through the laser communicator now slung at his belt again. To focus on the satellite from here, he'd had to aim just over the top of the House of Grace. . . .

"When the soldiers from Two come, there'll be a spark, won't there?" she asked. She was looking at Tyl now, though he didn't expect she could see any more of his face in the darkness than he could of her. Firelight winked on her necklace of translucent beads.

The scent she wore brought another momentary rush of lust.

"Maybe not," he said, comfortable talking to somebody who might possibly believe the story he

could never credit in discussions with himself.
"Nobody really wants that kind a' trouble."

Not the army, that was for sure. *They* weren't
going to push things.

"Delcorio makes a few concessions—he already
gave 'em Berne, after all. The troops march around
with their bayonets all polished to look pretty.
And then everybody kisses and makes up."

So that Tyl Koopman could get back to the
business of a war whose terms he understood.

"I hope . . ." Anne was murmuring.

She might not have finished the phrase even if
they hadn't been interrupted by the door sliding
open behind them.

Tyl didn't recognize Eunice Delcorio at first.
She was wearing a dress of mottled gray tones and
he'd only seen her in scarlet in the past. With the
fabric's luminors powered-up, the garment would
have shone with a more-than-metallic luster; but
now it had neither shape nor color, and Eunice's
voice glittered like that of a brittle ghost as she
said, "Well, my dear, I wouldn't have interrupted
you if I'd known you were entertaining a gentleman."

"Ma'am," Tyl said, bracing to attention. Eunice
sounded playful, but so was a cat with a field
mouse—and he didn't *know* what she could do to
him if she wanted, it wasn't in the normal chain of
command. . . .

"Captain Koopman and I were discussing the
situation, Eunice," Anne said evenly. If she were
embarrassed, she hid the fact; and there was no
trace of fear in her voice. "You could have called
me."

Eunice toyed with the hundred-millimeter wand
that could either page or track a paired unit. "I
thought I'd find you instead, my dear," she said.

The President's wife wasn't angry, but there was fierce emotion beneath the surface sparkle. The wand slipped from her fingers to the floor.

Tyl knelt swiftly—you don't bend when you're wearing a ceramic back-and-breast—and rose as quickly with the wand offered in his left hand.

Eunice batted the little device out into the courtyard. It was some seconds before it hit the stones below.

"I told the captain," Anne said evenly, "that I was concerned about your safety in view of the trouble that's occurring here in the city."

"Well, that should be over very shortly, shouldn't it?" Eunice said. Nothing in her voice hinted at the way her body had momentarily lost control. "Marshall Dowell has gone to Two himself to expedite movement of the troops."

The technical phrase came from her full lips with a glitter that made it part of a social event.

Which, in a manner of speaking, it was.

"Blood and Martyrs," Tyl said. He wasn't sure whether or not he'd spoken the curse aloud, and at this point he didn't much care.

He straightened. "Ma'am," he said, nodding stiffly to the President's wife. "Ah, ma'am," with a briefer nod to Anne.

He strode back into the building without waiting for formal leave. Over his shoulder, he called, "I need to go check on the dispositions of my troops."

Especially the troops out there with Desoix, in a city that the local army had just abandoned to the rebels.

CHAPTER NINETEEN

There were at least a dozen voices in the street outside, bellowing the bloodiest hymn Charles Desoix had ever heard. They were moving on, strolling if not marching, but the five Slammers kept their guns trained on the door in case somebody tried to join them inside the warehouse.

What bothered Desoix particularly was the clear soprano voice singing the descant, "Sew their manhood to our flags. . . ."

"All right," he said, returning his attention to the business of reconnecting the fusion powerplant which had been shut down for shipping. "Switch on."

Nothing happened.

Desoix, half inside the gun carriage's rear access port, straightened to find out what was happening. Lachere, the clerk he'd brought along because he needed another pair of hands, leaned hopefully from the open driver's compartment forward. "It's on, sir," he said.

"Main *and* Start-up are on?" Desoix demanded.

And either because they hadn't been or because a contact had been a little sticky, he heard the purr of the fusion bottle beginning to bring up its internal temperature and pressure.

Success. In less than an hour—

"The representative of Hammer's Regiment has an urgent message," said Control's emotionless voice. "Shall I patch him through?"

"Affirmative," Desoix said, blanking his mind so that it wouldn't flash him a montage of disaster as it always did when things were tight and the unexpected occurred.

Wouldn't show him Anne McGill in the arms of a dozen rioters, not dead yet and not to die for a long time. . . .

"We got a problem," Koopman said, as if his flat voice and the fact of his call hadn't already proved that. "Dowell just did a bunk to Two. I don't see the situation holding twenty-four hours. Over."

Maybe not twenty-four minutes.

"Is the Executive Guard . . ." Desoix began.

While he paused to choose his phrasing, Koopman interrupted with, "They're still here, but they're all in their quarters with the corridor blocked. I figure they're taking a vote. It's that sorta outfit. And I don't figure the vote's going any way I'd want it to. Over."

"All right," Desoix said, glancing toward the pressure gauge that he couldn't read in this light anyway. "All right, we'll have the gun drivable in thirty, that's three-oh, minutes. We'll—"

"Negative. Negative."

"Listen," the UDB officer said with his tone sharpening. "We're this far and we're not—"

Kekkonan, the sergeant in charge of the detachment of Slammers, tapped Desoix's elbow for attention and shook his head. "He said negative," Kekkonan said. "Sir."

The sergeant was getting the full conversation through his mastoid implant. Desoix didn't have to experiment to know it would be as much use to argue with a block of mahogany as with the dark, flat face of the non-com.

"Go ahead, Tyl," Desoix said with an inward sigh. "Over."

"You're not going to drive a calliope through the streets tonight, Charles," Koopman said. "Come dawn, maybe you can withdraw the one you got down there, maybe you just spike it and pull your guys out. This is save-what-you-got time, friend. And *my* boys aren't going to be part a' some fool stunt that sparks the whole thing off."

Kekkonan nodded. Not that he had to.

"Roger, we're on the way," Desoix said. He didn't have much emotion left to give the words, because his thoughts were tied up elsewhere.

Via, she was *married*. It was her bloody husband's business to take care of her, wasn't it?

CHAPTER TWENTY

"Go," said Desoix without emphasis.

Kekkonan and another of the Slammers flared from the door in opposite directions. Their cloaks—civilian and of neutral colors, green and gray—fluffed widely over their elbows, hiding the submachineguns in their hands.

"Clear," muttered Kekkonan. Desoix stepped out in the middle of the small unit. He felt as much a burden to his guards as the extra magazines that draped them beneath the loose garments.

It remained to be seen if either he or the ammunition would be of any service as they marched back to the Palace.

"Don't remember *that*," Lachere said, looking to the west.

"Keep moving," Kekkonan grunted. There was enough tension in his voice to add a threat of violence to the order.

One of the warehouses farther down the corniche—half a kilometer—had been set on fire. The flames reflected pink from the clouds and as a bloody froth from sea foam in the direction of Nevis Island. The boulevard was clogged by rioters watching the fire and jeering as they flung bodies into it.

Desoix remembered the descant, but he clasped Lachere's arm and said, "We weren't headed in that direction anyway, were we?"

"Too bloody right," murmured one of the Slammers, the shudder in his tone showing that he didn't feel any better about this than the UDB men did.

"Sergeant," Desoix said, edging close to Kekkonan and wishing that the two of them shared a command channel. "I think the faster we get off the seafront, the better we'll be."

He nodded toward the space between the warehouse they'd left and the next building—not so much an alley as a hedge against surveyors' errors.

"Great killing ground," Kekkonan snorted.

Flares rose from the plaza and burst in metallic showers above the city. Shots followed, tracers and the cyan flicker of powergun bolts aimed at the drifting sparks. There was more shooting, some of it from building roofs. Rounds curved in flat arcs back into the streets and houses.

A panel in the clear reflection of the House of Grace shattered into a rectangular scar.

"Right you are," said Kekkonan as he stepped into the narrow passage.

They had to move in single file. Desoix saw to it that he was the second man in the squad. Nobody objected.

He'd expected Tyl to give him infantrymen.

Instead, all five of these troopers came from vehicle crews, tanks and combat cars. The weapon of
choice under this night's conditions was a submachinegun, not the heavier, 2 cm semi-automatic
shoulder weapon of Hammer's infantry. Koopman
or his burly sergeant major had been thinking
when they picked this team.

Desoix's submachinegun wasn't for show either.
Providing air defense for front-line units meant
you were right in the middle of it when things
went wrong . . . and they'd twice gone wrong
very badly to a battery Charles Desoix crewed or
captained.

Though it shouldn't come to that. The seven of
them were just another group in a night through
which armed bands stalked in a truce that would
continue so long as there was an adequacy of
weaker prey.

The warehouses fronted the bay and the spaceport across the channel, but their loading docks
were in the rear. Across the mean street were
tenements. When Desoix's unit shrugged its way
out of the cramped passage, they found every one
of the windows facing them lighted to display a
cross as large as the sashes would allow.

"Party time," one of the troopers muttered.

Some of the residents were watching the events
from windows or rooftops, but most of them were
down in the street in amorphous clots like those of
white cells surrounding bacteria. There were shouts,
both shrill and guttural, but Desoix couldn't dis-
tinguish any of the words.

Not that he had any trouble understanding what
was going on without hearing the words. There
were screams coming from the center of one of
the groups . . . or perhaps Desoix's mind created

the sound it knew would be there if the victim
still had the strength to make it.

A dozen or so people were on the loading dock
to the unit's right, drinking and either having sex
or making as good an attempt at it as their drinking permitted. Somebody threw a bottle that
smashed close enough to Kekkonan that the sergeant's cloak flapped as he turned; but there didn't
appear to have been real malice involved. Perhaps
not even notice.

Party time.

"All right," Kekkonan said just loudly enough
for the soldiers with him to hear. "There's an alley
across the way, a little to the left. Stay loose, don't
run . . . and *don't* bunch up, just in case. Go."

Except for Lachere, they were all veterans; but
they were human as well. They didn't run, but
they moved much faster than the careless saunter
everybody knew was really the safest pace.

And they stayed close, close enough that one
burst could have gotten them all.

Nothing happened except that a score of voices
followed them with varied suggestions, and a
woman naked to the waist stumbled into Charles
Desoix even though he tried his best to dodge
her.

She was so drunk that she didn't notice the
contact, much less that she'd managed to grab the
muzzle of his submachinegun for an instant before
she caromed away.

The alley stank of all the garbage the rains
hadn't washed away; somebody, dead drunk or
dead, was sprawled just within the mouth of it.

Desoix had never been as eager to enter a bedroom as he was that alley.

"Ah, sir," one of the Slammers whispered as the

foetor and its sense of protection enclosed them. "Those people, they was rag-heads?"

The victims, he meant; and he was asking Desoix because Desoix was an officer who might know about things like that.

The Lord knew he did.

"Maybe," Desoix said.

They had enough room here to walk two abreast, though the lightless footing was doubtful and caused men to bump. "Landlords—building superintendents. The guy you owe money to, the guy who screwed your daughter and then married the trollop down the hall."

"But . . . ?" another soldier said.

"Anybody you're quick enough to point a dozen of your neighbors at," Desoix explained forcefully. "Before he points them at you. Party time."

The alley was the same throughout its length, but its other end opened onto more expensive facades and, across the broad street, patches of green surrounding the domed mass of the cathedral.

Traffic up the steps to the cathedral's arched south entrance was heavy and raucous. The street was choked by ground vehicles, some of them trying to move but even these blocked by the many which had been parked in the travel lanes.

"Hey there!" shouted the bearded leader of the group striding from the doorway just to the left of the alley. He wore two pistols in belt holsters; the cross on the shoulder of his red cape was perfunctory. "Where 're *you* going?"

"Back!" said Kekkonan over his shoulder, twisting to face the sudden threat.

Even before the one-syllable order was spoken, the torchlight and echoing voices up the alley behind them warned the unit that they couldn't retreat the way they had come without shooting their way through.

Which would leave them in a street with five hundred or a thousand aroused residents who had pretty well used up their local entertainment.

"Hey!" repeated the leader. The gang that had exited the building behind him were a dozen more of the same, differing only in sex, armament, and whether or not they carried open bottles.

Most of them did.

They'd seen Kekkonan's body armor—and maybe his gun—when he turned toward them.

"Hey," Desoix said cheerfully as he stepped in front of the sergeant. "You know us. We're soldiers."

He'd been stationed in Bamberg City long enough that his Spanish had some of the local inflections that weren't on the sleep-learning cube. He wouldn't pass for a local, but neither did his voice put him instantly in the foreign—victim—category to these thugs.

"From the Palace?" asked the leader. His hand was still on a pistol, but his face had relaxed because Desoix was relaxed.

Desoix wasn't sure his legs were going to hold him up. He'd been this frightened before, but that was when he was under fire and didn't have anything to do except crouch low and swear he'd resign and go home if only the Lord let him live this once.

"Sure," he said aloud, marveling at how well his voice worked. "Say, chickie—got anything there for a thirsty man?"

"Up your ass with it!" a red-caped female shrieked in amazement.

All the men in the group bellowed laughter.

One of them offered Desoix a flask of excellent wine, an off-planet vintage as good as anything served in the Palace.

"You're comin' to the cathedral, then?" the leader said as Desoix drank, tasting the liquid but feeling nothing. "Well, come on, then. The meeting's started by now or I'll be buggered."

"Not by me, Easton!" one of his henchmen chortled.

"Come on, boys," Desoix called, waving his unit out of the alley before there was a collision with the mob following. "We're already late for the meeting!"

Thank the Lord, the troopers all had the discipline or common sense to obey without question. Hemmed by the gang they'd joined perforce, surrounded by hundreds of other citizens wearing crosses over a variety of clothing, Desoix's unit tramped meekly up the steps of the cathedral.

Just before they entered the building, Desoix took the risk of muttering into his epaulet mike, "Tyl, we're making a necessary detour, but we're still coming back. If the Lord is with us, we're still coming back."

CHAPTER TWENTY-ONE

The nave was already full. Voices echoing in debate showed that the gang leader had been correct about the meeting having started. Hospital orderlies with staves guarded the entrance—keeping order rather than positioned to stop an attack.

Bishop Trimer and those working with him knew there would be no attack—until they gave the order.

Easton blustered, but there was no bluffing the white-robed men blocking the doorway. One of the orderlies spoke into a radio with a belt-pack power source, while the man next to him keyed a hand-held computer. A hologram of the bearded thug bloomed atop the computer in green light.

"Right, Easton," the guard captain said. "Left stairs to the north gallery. You and your folks make any trouble, we'll deal with it. Throw anything into the nave and you'll all decorate lamp posts. Understood?"

"Hey, I'm important!" the gang boss insisted. "I speak for the whole Seventeenth Ward, and I belong down with the bosses on the floor!"

"Right now, you belong on the Red side of the gallery," said the orderly. "Or out on your butts. Take your pick."

"You'll regret this!" Easton cried as he shuffled toward the indicated staircase. "I got friends! I'll make it hot fer you!"

"Who're you?" the guard captain asked Charles Desoix. His face was as grizzled as that of the Slammers sergeant major; his eyes were as flat as death.

If Desoix hadn't seen the platoon of orderlies with assault rifles rouse from the ante-chamber when the gang boss threatened, he would have been tempted to turn back down the steps instead of answering. He couldn't pick his choice of realities, though.

"We're soldiers," he said, leaving the details fuzzy as he had before. "Ah—this isn't official, we aren't, you see. We just thought we'd, ah . . . be ready ourselves to do our part . . . ."

He hoped that meant something positive to the guard captain, without sounding *so* positive that they'd wind up in the middle of real trouble.

The fellow with the radio was speaking into it as his eyes locked with Desoix's. The UDB officer smiled brightly. The guard captain was talking to another of his men while both of them also looked at Desoix.

"All right," the captain said abruptly. "There's plenty of room in the south gallery. We're glad to

have more converts to the ranks of active righte-
ousness."

"We shoulda bugged out," muttered one of the
troopers as they mounted the helical stairs behind
Desoix.

"Keep your trap shut and do what the el-tee
says," Sergeant Kekkonan snarled back.

For good or ill, Charles Desoix was in command
now.

Given the sophistication of the commo unit the
orderly at the door held, Desoix didn't dare try to
report anything useful to those awaiting him back
in the Palace. He hoped Anne would have had
sense enough to flee the city before he got back to
the Palace.

Almost as much as another part of him prayed
that she would be waiting when he returned; because he was very badly going to need the relax-
ation she brought him.

CHAPTER TWENTY-TWO

In daytime the dome would have floated on sunlight streaming through the forty arched windows on which it was supported. The hidden floods directed from light-troughs to reflect from the inner surface were harsh and metallic by contrast, even though the metal was gold.

Desoix and his unit muscled their way to the railing of colored marble overlooking the nave. It might have been smarter to hang back against the gallery windows, but they were big men and aggressive enough to have found a career in institutionalized murder.

They were standing close to the east end and the hemicycle containing the altar, where the major figures in the present drama now faced the crowd of their supporters and underlings.

Between the two groups was a line of orderlies kneeling shoulder to shoulder. Even by leaning over the rail, Desoix could not see the faces of those on the altar dais.

But there were surprises in the crowd.

"That's Cerulio," Desoix said, nudging Kekkonan to look at a sumptuously dressed man in the front rank. His wife was with him, and the four men in blue around them were surely liveried servants. "He was in the Palace an hour ago. Said he was going to check his townhouse, but that he'd be back before morning."

"Don't know him," grunted Kekkonan. "But that one, three places over—" he didn't point, which reminded Desoix that pointing called attention to both ends of the outstretched arm "—he's in the adjutant general's staff, a colonel I'm pretty sure. Saw him when we were trying to requisition bunks."

Desoix felt a chill all the way up his spine. Though it didn't change anything beyond what they had already determined this night.

The man speaking wore white and a mitre, so that even from above there could be no mistaking Bishop Trimer.

"—wither away," his voice was saying. "Only in the last resort would God have us loose the righteous indignation that this so-called president has aroused in our hearts, in the heart of every Christian on Bamberia."

One shot, thought Charles Desoix.

He couldn't see Trimer's face, but there was a line of bare neck visible between mitre and chasuble. No armor there, no way to staunch the blood when a cyan bolt blasts a crater the size of a clenched fist.

And no way for the small group of soldiers to avoid being pulled into similarly fist-sized gobbets when the mob took its revenge in the aftermath. "Not our fight," Desoix muttered to himself.

He didn't have to explain that to any of his companions. He was pretty sure that Sergeant Kekkonan would kill him in an eye-blink if he thought the UDB officer was about to sacrifice them all.

"We will wait a day, in God's name," the Bishop said. He was standing with his arms outstretched.

Trimer had a good voice and what was probably a commanding manner to those who didn't see him from above—like Charles Desoix and God, assuming God was more than a step in Bishop Trimer's pursuit of temporal power. He could almost have filled the huge church with his unaided voice, and the strain of listening would have quieted the crowd that was restive with excitement and drink.

As it was, Trimer's words were relayed through hundreds of speakers hidden in the pendentives and among the acanthus leaves of the column capitals. Multiple sources echoed and fought one another, creating a busyness that encouraged whispering and argument among the audience.

Desoix had been part of enough inter-unit staff meetings to both recognize and explain the strain that was building in the Bishop's voice. Trimer was used to being in charge; and here, in his own cathedral, circumstances had conspired to rob him of the absolute control he normally exercised.

The man seated to Trimer's right got up. Like the Bishop, he was recognizable by his clothing—a red cape and a red beret in which a bird plume of some sort bobbed when he moved his head.

The Bishop turned. The gallery opposite Desoix exploded with cheers and cat-calls. Red-garbed spectators in the nave below were jumping, making their capes balloon like bubbles boiling through a thick red sauce, despite the efforts of the hospital orderlies keeping the two factions separate.

All the men on the dais were standing with their hands raised. The noise lessened, then paused in a great hiss that the pillared aisles drank.

"Ten minutes each, we agreed," one of the faction leaders said to the Bishop in a voice amplified across the whole cathedral.

"Speak, then!" said the Bishop in a voice that was short of being a snarl by as little as the commotion below had avoided being a full-fledged riot.

Trimer and most of the others on the dais seated themselves again, leaving the man in red to stand alone. There was more cheering and, ominously, boos and threats from Desoix's side of the hall. Around the soldiers, orderlies fought a score of violent struggles with thugs in black.

The man in red raised his hands again and boomed, "Everybody siddown, curse it! We're *friends* here, friends—"

When the sound level dropped minusculy, he added, "Rich friends we're gonna be, every one of us!"

The cheers were general loud enough to make the light troughs wobble.

"Now all you know there's no bigger supporter of the Bishop than I am," the gang boss continued in a voice whose nasality was smoothed by the multiple echoes. "But there's something else you all know, too. I'm not the man to back off when I got the hammer on some bastid neither."

He wasn't a stupid man. He forestalled the cheers—and the threats from the opposing side of the great room—that would have followed the statement by waving his arms again for silence even as he spoke.

"Now the way I sees it," he went on. "The way *anybody* sees it—is we got the hammer on Delcorio. So right now's the time we break 'is bloody neck for 'im. Not next week or next bloody year when somebody's cut another deal with 'im and he's got the streets full a' bloody soldiers!"

In the tumult of agreement, Desoix saw a woman wearing black cross-belts fight her way to the front of the spectators' section and wave a note over the heads of the line of orderlies.

The black-caped gang boss looked a question to the commo-helmeted aide with him on the dais. The aide shrugged in equal doubt, then obeyed the nodded order to reach across the orderlies and take the note from the woman's hand.

"Now the Bishop says," continued the man in red, " 'give him a little time, he'll waste right away and nobody gets hurt.' And that's fine, sure . . . but maybe it's time a few a' them snooty bastids *does* get hurt, right?"

The shouts of *yes* and *kill* were punctuated with other sounds as bestial as the cries of panthers hunting. It was noticeable that the front rank of spectators, the men and women with estates and townhouses, either sat silent or looked about nervously as they tried to feign enthusiasm.

While the red leader waited with his head thrown back and arms akimbo, the rival gang boss read the note he had been passed. He reached toward Bishop Trimer with it and, when another priest tried to take the document from his hand, swatted the man away. Trimer leaned over to read the note.

"Now I say," the man in red resumed in a lull, "all right, we give Delcorio time. We give the bastid as much time as it takes fer us to march over to the Palace and pull it down—"

The black-caped gang boss got up, drawing the Bishop's gaze to follow the note being thrust at the leader of the other street gang.

The timbre of the shouting changed as the spectators assessed what was happening in their own terms—and prepared for the immediate battle those terms might entail.

"The rightful President of Bamberia is Thomas Chastain," cried the black-caped leader as the cathedral hushed and his rival squinted at the note in the red light.

The man in red looked up but did not interrupt as the other leader thundered in a deep bass, "He was robbed of his heritage by the Delcorios and held under their guards in the Palace—but now he's escaped! Thom Chastain's at his house right now, waiting for us to come and restore him to his position!"

Everyone on the dais was standing. Some of the leaders, Church and gangs and surely the business community as well, tried to speak to one another over the tumult. Unless they could read lips, that was a useless exercise.

Desoix was sure of that. He'd been caught in an artillery barrage, and the decibel level of the bursting shells had been no greater than that of the voices reverberating now in the cathedral.

Bishop Trimer touched the gang bosses. They conferred with looks, then stepped back to give the Bishop the floor again. Though they did not sit down, they motioned their subordinates into chairs on the dais. After a minute or two, the room had quieted enough for Trimer to speak.

"My people," he began with his arms outstretched in benediction. "You have spoken, and the Lord God has made his will known to us. We will gather at dawn here—"

The gang bosses had been whispering to one another. The man in black tugged the Bishop's arm firmly enough to bring a burly priest—Father Laughlin?—from his seat. Before he could intervene, the red-garbed leader spoke to Trimer with forceful gestures of his hand.

The Bishop nodded. Desoix couldn't see his face, but he could imagine the look of bland agreement wiped thinly over fury at being interrupted and dictated to by thugs.

"My people," he continued with unctuous warmth, "we will meet at dawn in the plaza, where all the city can see me anoint our rightful president in the name of God who rules us. Then we will carry President Chastain with us to the Palace to claim his seat—and God will strengthen our arms to smite anyone so steeped in sin that they would deny his will. At dawn!"

The cheering went on and on. Even in the gallery, where the floor and the pillars of colored marble provided a screen from the worst of the noise, it was some minutes before Kekkonan could shout into Desoix's ear, "What's that mean for us, sir?"

"It means," the UDB officer shouted back, "that we've got a couple hours to load what we can and get the hell out of Bamberg City."

He paused a moment, then added, "It means we've had a good deal more luck the past half hour than we had any right to expect."

CHAPTER TWENTY-THREE

"We got 'em in sight," said Scratchard's voice through Tyl's commo helmet. The sergeant major was on the roof with the ten best marksmen in the unit. "Everybody together, no signs they're being followed."

Tyl started to acknowledge, but before he could Scratchard concluded, "Plenty units out tonight besides them, but nobody seems too interested in them nor us. Over."

"Over and out," Tyl said, letting his voice stand for his identification.

He locked eyes with the sullen Guards officer across the doorway from him, Captain Sanchez, and said, "Open it up, sir. I got a team coming in."

There were two dozen soldiers in the rotunda: the ordinary complement of Executive Guards and the squad Tyl had brought with him when Desoix blipped that they were clear again and heading in.

Earlier that night, the UDB officer had talked Tyl and his men through the doors that might have been barred to them. Tyl wasn't at all sure his diplomacy was good enough for him to return the favor diplomatically.

But he didn't doubt the locals would accept any suggestion he chose to make with a squad of Slammers at his back.

Sanchez didn't respond, but the man at the shutter controls punched the right buttons instantly. Warm air, laced with smoke more pungent than that of the omnipresent cigars, puffed into the circular hall.

Tyl stepped into the night.

The height and width of the House of Grace was marked by a cross of bluish light, a polarized surface discharge from the vitril glazing. It was impressive despite being marred by several shattered panels.

And it was the only light in the city beyond handcarried lanterns and the sickly pink-orange-red of spreading fires. Street lights that hadn't been cut when transformers shorted were tempting targets for gunmen.

So were lighted windows, now that the meeting in the cathedral had broken up and the gangs were out in force again.

Tyl clicked his faceshield down in the lighted courtyard and watched the seven soldiers jogging toward him with the greenish tinge of enhanced ambient light.

"All present 'n accounted for, sir," muttered Kekkonan when he reached Tyl, reporting because he was the senior Slammer in the unit.

"Sergeant major's got a squad on the roof," Tyl
explained. "Make sure your own gear's ready to
move, then relieve Jack. All right?"

"Yes *sir*," said Kekkonan and ducked off after
his men. The emotion in his agreement was the
only hint the non-com gave of just how tight things
had been an hour before.

"Lachere, make sure Control's core pack's ready
to jerk out," Desoix said. "We've got one jeep, so
don't expect to leave with more than you can carry
walking."

The clerk's boots skidded on the rotunda's stone
flooring as he scampered to obey.

Desoix put his arm around Tyl's shoulders as
they followed their subordinates through armored
doors which the guard immediately began to close
behind them. Tyl was glad of the contact. He felt
like a rat in a maze in this warren of corridors and
blocked exits.

"I appreciate your help," Desoix said. "It might
have worked. And without those very good people
you lent me, it would—"

He paused. "It wouldn't have been survivable.
And I'd have probably made the attempt anyway,
because I didn't understand what it was like out
there until we started back."

"I guess . . ." Tyl said. "I guess we better
report to, to the President before we go. Unless
he was tapping the push. I guess we owe him
that, for the contract."

They stepped together into the small elevator.
It was no longer separately guarded. The Executive Guardsmen watched them without expression.

A few of the Slammers stationed in the rotunda
threw ironic salutes. They were in a brighter mood
than they'd been a few minutes before. They knew

from their fellows who'd just come in that the whole unit would be bugging out shortly.

"You're short of transport too?" Tyl asked, trying to keep the concern out of his voice as he watched Desoix sidelong.

"I can give my seat to your sergeant major, if that's what you mean," Desoix replied. "I've hiked before. But yes, this was the base unit they robbed to outfit all the batteries on Two that had to be mobile."

That was exactly what Tyl had meant.

The elevator stopped. In the moment before the door opened, Desoix added, "There's vehicles parked in the garage under the Palace here. If we're providing protection, there shouldn't be a problem arranging rides."

If it's safe to call attention to yourself with a vehicle, Tyl thought, remembering the fire trucks. Luxury cars with the presidential seal would be even better targets.

Tyl expected Anne McGill to be at the open door connecting the Consistory Room with the presidential suite, where she could be in sight of her mistress and still able to hear the elevator arrive. She was closer than that, arm's length of the elevator—and so was Eunice Delcorio.

The President was across the room, in silhouette against the faint flow which was all that remained of the City Offices toward which he was staring. His nephew stood beside him, but there was no one else—not even a servant—in the darkened room.

"Charles?" Anne said. Her big body trembled like a spring, but she did not reach to clasp her lover now, in front of Eunice.

Tyl let Desoix handle the next part. They hadn't

discussed it, but the UDB officer knew more about things like this . . . politics and the emotions that accompany politics.

Desoix stepped forward and bowed to Eunice Delcorio, expertly sweeping back the civilian cape he still wore over his gun and armor. "Madam," he said. "Sir—" John Delcorio had turned to watch them, though he remained where he was. "I very much regret that it's time for you to withdraw from the city."

The President slammed the bottom of his fist against the marble pillar beside him. Anne was nodding hopeful agreement; her mistress was still, though not calm.

"There's still time to get out," Desoix continued.

Tyl marveled at Desoix's control. *He* wanted to get out, wanted it so badly that he had to consciously restrain himself from jumping into the elevator and ordering the unit to form on him in the courtyard.

"But *barely* enough time. The—they are going to anoint Thom Chastain President at dawn in the plaza, and then they'll come here. Even if they haven't gotten heavy weapons from one of the military arsenals, there's no possible way that the Palace can be defended."

"I knew the swine were betraying me," Delcorio shouted. "I should never have let them live, never!"

"We can cover the way out if you move fast enough," Tyl said aloud. "Ten minutes, maybe."

What he'd seen in the Consistory Room and heard from Desoix's terse report on the way back to the Palace convinced him that Delcorio, not Thom Chastain, was responsible for the present situation. But *why* didn't matter any more.

"All right," the President said calmly. "I've al-

ready packed the seal and robes of state. I had to
do it myself because they'd all run, even Hein-
rich. . . ."

"No," said Eunice Delcorio. "*No!*"

"Eunice," begged Anne McGill.

"Ma'am," said Tyl Koopman desperately. "There's
no way."

He was unwilling to see people throw themselves away. You learn that when you fight for
hire. There's always another contract, if you're
around to take it up. . . .

"I've been mistress of this city, of this planet,"
the President's wife said in a voice that hummed
like a cable being tightened. "If they think to
change that, well, they can burn me in the Palace
first."

She turned to stare, either at her husband or at
the smoldering night beyond him. "It'll be a fitting monument, I think," she said.

"And I'll set the fires *myself*—" whirling, her
eyes lashed both the mercenary officers "—if no
one's man enough to help me defend it."

Anne McGill fell to her knees, praying or crying.

"Madam," said Major Borodin, entering from
the hall unannounced because there was no greeter
in the building to announce him.

The battery commander looked neither nervous
nor frustrated. There was an aura of vague distaste
about him, the way his sort of officer always looked
when required to speak to a group of people.

This was a set speech, not a contribution to the
discussion.

"I urge you," Borodin went on, reeling the
words off a sheaf of mental notes, "to use common
sense in making personal decisions. So far as public decisions go, I must inform you that I am

withdrawing my battery from the area affected by the present unrest, under orders of my commander —and with the concurrence of our legal staff."

"I said—" John Delcorio began, ready to blaze up harmlessly at having his nose rubbed in a reality of which he was already aware.

"No, of *course* we can defeat them!" said Eunice, pirouetting to Borodin's side with a girlish sprightliness that surprised everyone else in the room as much as it did the major.

"No, no," the President's wife continued brightly, one hand on Borodin's elbow while the other hand gestured to her audience. "It's really quite possible, don't you see? There's many of them and only a few of us—but if they're in the plaza, well, we just hold the entrances."

She stroked Borodin's arm and waved, palm up, to Tyl and Desoix. Her smile seemed to double the width of her face. "You brave lads can do that, can't you? Just the three stairs, and you'll have the Executive Guard to help you. The Bishop won't make any trouble about coming to the Palace alone to discuss matters if the choice is. . . ."

Eunice paused delicately. This wasn't the woman who moments before had been ready—*had* been ready—to burn herself alive with the Palace. "And this way, all the trouble ends and no one more gets hurt, all the rioting and troubles. . . ."

"No," said Major Borodin. His eyes were bulging and he didn't appear to be seeing any of his present surroundings. His mental notes had been hopelessly disarrayed by this—

"Yes, yes, of *course!*" President Delcorio said, rubbing his hands together in anticipation. "We'll see how much Trimer blusters when he's asked to come and there's a *gun* at his head to see that he does!"

Tyl had pointed enough guns to know that they weren't the kind of magic wand Delcorio seemed to be expecting. He looked at Desoix, certain of agreement and hopeful that the UDB officer would be able to express the plan's absurdity in a more tactful fashion than Tyl could.

Desoix had lifted Anne McGill to her feet. His hand was on the woman's waist, but she wasn't paying any conscious attention to him. Instead, her eyes were on Eunice Delcorio.

"No," muttered Borodin. "No, no! We've got to withdraw at once."

Maybe it was the rote dismissal by the battery commander that made Tyl really start thinking. Colonel Hammer wanted Delcorio kept in power for another week—and no deal Trimer cut with the present government was likely to last *longer* than that, but a week . . . ?

Two hundred men and a pair of calliopes—blazes, maybe it *would* work!

"Of course," Tyl said aloud, "Marshal Dowell's on the other side, sure as can be, so the Guard downstairs . . . ?"

"Dowell isn't the Executive Guard," said the President dismissively. "He's nothing but a jumped-up shopkeeper. I was a fool to think he'd be loyal because he owed everything to me."

Like City Prefect Berne, Tyl thought. He kept his mouth shut.

"But the Guard, they're the best people in the State," Delcorio continued with enthusiasm. "They won't give in to trash and gutter-sweepings now that we've found a way to deal with them."

"Lieutenant," said the battery commander, "I'll

oversee the loading. Give the withdrawal orders as soon as you've determined the safest routes."

He pivoted on his left heel, rotating his elbow from Eunice's seductive touch. He stamped out of the room.

"Yes sir," Desoix said crisply, but he made no immediate motion to follow his superior.

"Well," said Tyl, feeling the relief that returned with resignation—it'd been a crazy notion, but just for a minute he'd thought. . . . "Well, I better tell—"

"Wait!" Anne McGill said. She stepped toward her mistress, but she was no longer ignoring Charles Desoix. Halfway between the two she spun toward her lover and set a jewel-ringed hand at the scooped collar of the dress she wore beneath her cloak. She pulled fiercely.

The hem of lustrous synthetic held. White and red creases sprang out where the straps crossed her shoulders.

"Anne?" the President's wife called from behind her companion.

Anne wailed, "Mary, Queen of Heaven!" and tugged again, pulling the left strap down to her elbow instead of trying again to tear the fabric. Her breast, firm but far too heavy not to sag, flopped over the bodice which had restrained it.

"Is this what you want to give to them?" she cried. Her eyes were blind, even before she shut them in a vain attempt to hold back the tears. "Give the, the *mob*? I won't go! I won't leave Eunice even if you *are* all cowards!"

"Anne," Desoix pleaded. "President Delcorio—the front row in the cathedral *was* the best people in the State. Some of them were here with you this morning. Colonel Drescher isn't going to—"

"How do you know until you ask him?" Eunice demanded in a voice like a rapier. Her arm was around Anne McGill now, drawing the dark cloak over the naked breast. Tyl couldn't say whether the gesture was motherly or simply proprietary.

This hasn't got anything t' do with . . . his surface mind started to tell him; but deeper down, he knew it did. Like as not it always did, one way or another; who was screwing who and how everybody felt about it.

"All right!" Desoix shouted. "We'll go ask him!"

"I'll go myself," said President Delcorio, sucking in his belly and adding a centimeter to his height by straightening up.

"That's not safe, Uncle John," said Pedro Delcorio unexpectedly. "I'll go with the men."

"Well . . ." Tyl said as the President's nephew gestured him toward the elevator. Desoix, his face set in furious determination, was already inside.

It was going to be cramped with three of them.

"Via, why not?" Tyl said. It was easier to go along than to refuse to, right now. Nothing would come of it. He'd seen too many parade-ground units to expect this one to find guts all of a sudden.

But if just maybe it did work. . . . Via, *nobody* liked to run with their tail between their legs, did they?

CHAPTER TWENTY-FOUR

Koopman's idiotic grin was just one more irritation to Charles Desoix as the elevator dropped.

"Bit of a chance you're taking, isn't it?" the Slammers officer asked. "Going against your major's orders and all?"

Desoix felt himself become calm and was glad of it. None of this made any sense. If Tyl decided to laugh—well, that was a saner response than Desoix's own.

"Only if something comes of it," he said, wishing that he didn't sound so tired. Wrung out.

He *was* wrung out. "And if I'm alive afterward, of course."

Pedro's eyes were darting between the mercenaries. His bulky body—soft but not flabby—would have given him presence under some circumstances. In these tight quarters he was overwhelmed by the men in armor—and by the way they considered the future in the light of similar past.

The car settled so gently that only the door opening announced the rotunda. Desoix swung out to the left side, noticing that identical reflex had moved Koopman to the right—as if they were about to clear a defended position.

Half a dozen powerguns were leveled at the opening door, though the Slammers here on guard jerked their muzzles away when they saw who had arrived.

The rotunda was empty except for Hammer's men.

"Where's the guards?" Koopman demanded in amazement.

One of his men shrugged. "A few minutes back, they all moved out."

He pointed down the corridor that led toward the Guard billets. "I called the sar'ent major, but he said hold what we got, he and the rest a' the company'd be with us any time now."

"Let's go, then!" said Pedro Delcorio, trotting in the direction of the gesture.

Desoix followed, because that was what he'd set out to do. He hunched himself to settle his armor again. When he felt cold, as now, he seemed to shrink within the ceramic shell.

"Carry on," Koopman said to his guard squad. As the Slammers officer strode along behind the other two men, Desoix heard him speaking into his commo helmet in a low voice.

The barracks of the Executive Guard occupied the back corridor of the Palace's south wing. It had its own double gate of scissor-hinged brass bars over a panel of imported hardwood, both portions polished daily by servants.

The bars were open, the panel—steel-cored, Desoix now noticed—ajar. Captain Sanchez and the squad he'd commanded in the rotunda stood in the opening, arguing with other Guardsmen in the corridor beyond. When they heard the sound of boots approaching, they whirled. Several of them aimed their rifles.

Charles Desoix froze, raising his hands and moving them out from his sides. He had been close to death a number of times already this night.

But never closer than now.

"What do you men think you're doing?" Pedro demanded in a voice tremulous with rage. "Don't you recognize me? I'm—"

"*No!*" Sanchez snapped to the man at his side. The leveled assault rifle wavered but did not fire—as both Desoix and the Guards captain had expected.

"Wha . . . ?" Delcorio said in bewilderment.

"Rene, it's me," Desoix called in an easy voice. He sidled a step so that Sanchez could see him clearly past the President's nephew. Walking *forward* was possible suicide. "Charles, you know? We came to discuss the present situation with Colonel Drescher."

The words rolled off Desoix's tongue, amazing him with their blandness and fluency. Whatever else that scene upstairs with Anne had done, it had burned the capacity to be shocked out of him for a time.

Drescher stepped forward when his name was spoken. He had been the other half of the argument in the gateway. The lower ranking Guardsmen grounded their weapons as if embarrassed to be touching real hardware in the presence of their commander.

"Master Desoix," said Drescher, "we're very busy just now. I have nothing to discuss with you or any of John Delcorio's by-blows."

"*What*?" Pedro Delcorio shouted, able this time to get the full syllable out in his rage.

Koopman put a hand, his left hand, on the young civilian's shoulder and shifted him back a step without being too obvious about the force required.

Desoix walked forward, turning his spread arms into gestures as he said, "Sir, it's become possible to quell the rioting without further bloodshed or the need for additional troops. We'd like to discuss the matter with you for a moment."

As if Drescher's deliberate ignorance of his military rank didn't bother him, Desoix added with an ingratiating smile, "It will make you the hero of the day, sir. Of the century."

"And who's that?" Drescher said, waving his swagger stick in the direction of the Slammers officer. "Your trained dog, Desoix?"

Recent events had shocked the Guard Commandant into denial so deep that he was being more insulting than usual—to prove that civilization and the rule of law still maintained in his presence. Charles Desoix knew that, but Tyl Koopman with a submachinegun under his arm—

"No sir," said the Slammers officer. "I'm Captain Koopman of Hammer's Regiment. My unit's part of the defense team."

"Sir," Desoix said in the pause that followed Koopman's response and sudden awareness of what the mercenary's response *could* have been. "The mob will have gathered in the plaza by dawn. By sealing the three exits, we can bring their, ah, leaders, to a reasonable accommodation with the government."

"The government of the State," said Drescher icily, cutting through Desoix's planned next phrase, "is what God and the people choose it to be. The Executive Guard would not presume to interfere with that choice."

"Colonel," Desoix said. He could feel his eyes widening, but he didn't see the Guardsmen in front of him. In his mind, a dozen men were raping Anne McGill while shrill-voiced women urged them on. "If they attack the Palace, there'll be a bloodbath."

"Then it's necessary to evacuate the Palace, isn't it?" Drescher replied. "Now, if you *gentle*—"

"Don't you boys take oaths?" Koopman asked curiously. There wasn't any apparent emotion in his tone. "Don't they matter to you?"

Colonel Drescher went white. "You foreign mercenaries have a vision of Bamberg politics," he said, "that a native can only describe as bizarre." His voice sounded as though he would have been screaming if his lungs held enough air.

"Now get *away* from here!"

Charles Desoix bowed low. "Gentlemen," he murmured to his companions as he turned. "We have no further business here."

They didn't look behind them as they marched to where the corridor jogged and the wall gave them cover against a burst of shots into their backs. Pedro Delcorio was shaking.

So was Koopman, but it showed itself as a lilt in his voice as he said, "Well, they're frightened. Can't blame 'em, can we, Charles? And they'd not have been much use, just stand there and nobody who'd seen 'em in their prettiness was going to be much scared, eh?"

Adrenalin was babbling through the lips of the Slammers officer. His right hand was working in front of him where the Guardsmen couldn't see it, clenching and unclenching, because if it didn't move, it was going to find its home on the grip of his submachinegun. . . .

Anne was waiting around the corner. She looked at the faces of the three men and closed her eyes.

"Anne, we can't—" Desoix began. He was sure there had to be something he could say that would keep her from the suicide she'd threatened, at the hands of the mob or more abruptly here with a rope or the gun he knew she kept in her bedroom.

"Sure we can," said Tyl Koopman. His voice had no emotion, and his eyes had an eerie, thousand-meter stare.

"You've got a calliope aimed at both side-stairs, sure, they won't buck that, one burst and that's over. And me and the boys, sure, we'll take the main stairs, those lock gates, they're like vaults, *no* problem."

"Then it's all right?" Anne said in amazement. Her beautiful face was lighting as if she were watching a theophany. "You can still save us, Charles?"

She touched her fingertips to his chest, assuring herself of her lover's continuing humanity.

"I—" said Charles Desoix. He looked at the Slammers officer, then back into the eyes of Anne McGill.

They'd have to do something about Major Borodin—literally put the old man under restraint. Maybe Delcorio still had a few servants around who could handle that.

"I—" Desoix repeated.

Then he squared his shoulders and said, "Certainly, darling, Tyl and I can handle it without the help of *those* fools."

It amazed the UDB officer to realize how easily he had decided to ruin his life. The saving grace was the fact that there wouldn't be many hours of life remaining to him after this decision.

CHAPTER TWENTY-FIVE

Tyl watched the antenna of his laser communicator quest on the porch outside the Consistory Room, making a keening sound as it searched for its satellite. The link was still thirty seconds short of completion when his commo helmet said, "Four-six to Six, over."

Tyl jumped, ringing the muzzle of his submachine-gun against the rail as he spun.

"Go ahead, Four-six," he said to Sergeant Major Scratchard when he realized that the call was on the unit push, not the laser link he'd been setting up. He was a hair late in his response, but nobody else knew the unexpected call had scared him like that.

"Sir," said Scratchard, "the Palace troops, they're all marching out one a' the side doors right now. Over."

Good riddance, Tyl thought. "Let 'em go, Jack," he said. "Over and out."

"Six?"

"Go ahead, Four-six."

"Sir, should we secure the doors after them? Over."

"Negative, Four-six," Tyl snapped. "*Ignore* this bloody building and carry out your orders! Six out."

It hadn't been that silly a question. Jack was nervous because he didn't know much, because Tyl hadn't *told* him very much. The non-com was trying to cross all possible tees because he couldn't guess which ones would turn out to be of critical importance.

Neither could his captain. Which was the real reason Tyl had jumped down the sergeant major's throat.

A dim red light pulsed on the antenna's tracking head, indicating that the unit had locked on. Tyl switched modes on his helmet, grimaced, and said, "Koopman to Central, over."

Seconds of flickering static, aural and visual, took his mind off the cross dominating the skyline toward which the laser pointed. It was only an hour before dawn. The streets were alive with bands of men and women, ant-small at this distance and moving like foraging ants toward the plaza.

"Hold one," said the helmet. The screen surged into momentary crystal sharpness. Colonel Hammer glared from it.

He looked very tired. All but his eyes.

"Go ahead, Captain," Hammer said, and the static fuzzing his voice blurred his image a moment later as well, as though a bead curtain had been drawn between Tyl and his commander.

Tyl found that a lot more comfortable. Funny the things you worry about instead of the really worrisome things. . . .

"Sir," he said, knowing that his voice sounded dull—it had to, he couldn't let emotion get out during this report because he hadn't any idea of what emotion he'd find himself displaying. "I've alerted my men for an operation at dawn to bottle up the rioters and demand the surrender of their leaders. We'll be operating in concert with elements of the UDB."

There was no need to say "over," since the speakers could see one another—albeit with a lag of a few seconds. Tyl keyed the thumb-sized unit on his sending head, a module loaded with the street plan, routes, and make-up of the units taking part in the operation. The pre-load burped out like an angry katydid.

Hammer's eyes, never at rest, paused briefly on a point to the left of the pick-up feeding Tyl's screen. A separate holotank was displaying the schematic, while Tyl's face continued to fill the main unit.

Hammer's face wore no expression as it clicked to meet Tyl's eyes again. "What are the numbers on the other side?" he asked emotionlessly.

"Sir, upwards of twenty kay. Maybe fifty, the plaza'd hold that much and more."

Tyl paused. "Sir," he added, "we can't fight 'em, we know that. But maybe we can face them down, the leaders."

People were moving in the courtyard beneath him, four cloaked figures slipping out of the Palace on their missions. Desoix and his two clerks to the

warehouse and the calliope they'd set up only
hours before. And. . .

"How are you timing your assault?" the Colonel asked calmly. "If the ringleaders aren't
present, you've gained nothing. And if you wait
too long. . . ?"

"Sir, one of the women from the Palace," Tyl
explained. "She's, ah, getting in position right
now in the south gallery of the cathedral. There's
a view to the altar on the seafront, that's where
the big ones 'll be. She'll cue us when she spots
the ones we need."

He thought he was done speaking, but his tongue
went on unexpectedly, "Sir, we thought of using a
man, but a woman going to pray now—it's not
going to upset anything. She'll be all right."

The Colonel frowned as if trying to understand
why a line captain was apologizing for using a
female look-out. It didn't make a lot of sense to
Tyl either, after he heard his own words—but
he'd been away for a long time.

And anyway, the only similarity between Anne
McGill and the dozen females in Tyl's present
command was that their plumbing was the same.

"What happens if they don't back down?" Hammer said in a voice like a whetstone, apparently
smooth but certain to wear away whatever it rubs
against, given time and will.

"We bug out," Tyl answered frankly. "The mall
at the main stairs, that's where we'll be, it's got
gates like bank vaults on all four sides. Things
don't work out, Trimer ducks instead of putting
his hands up and his buddies start shooting—well,
we slam the plaza-side doors and we're gone."

"And your supports?" Hammer asked. His mouth

wavered in what might have been either static or an incipient grin.

"Desoix's men, they're mounted," Tyl said. It was an open question whether or not you could really load a double crew on a calliope and drive away with it, but that was one for the UDB to answer. "Worst case, there's going to be too much confusion for organized pursuit. Unless. . ."

"Unless the streets are already blocked behind you," said Colonel Hammer, who must have begun speaking before Tyl's voice trailed off on the same awareness. "Unless there's a large enough group of rioters between your unit and safety to hold you for their fifty thousand friends to arrive."

"Yes sir," said Tyl.

He swallowed. "Sir," he said, "I can't promise it'll work. If it does, it'll give you the time you wanted for things to hot up over there. But I can't promise."

"Son," said Colonel Hammer. He was grinning like a skull. "When you start making promises on chances like this, I'll remove you from command so fast your ears 'll ring."

His face straightened into neutral lines again. "For the record," Hammer said, "you're operating without orders. Not in violation of orders, just on your own initiative."

"Yes *sir*," Tyl said.

Hammer hadn't paused for agreement. He was saying, "I expect you to withdraw as soon as you determine that there is no longer a realistic chance of success. Nobody's being paid to be heroes, and—"

He leaned closer to the pick-up. His face was grim and his eyes glared like gun muzzles. "Captain, if you throw my men away because *you* want to be a hero, I'll shoot you with my own hand. If you survive."

"Yes *sir*," Tyl said through a swallow. This time his commander *had* waited for an acknowledgment.

Hammer softened. "Then good luck to you, son," he said. "Oh—and son?"

"Yes sir?"

The Colonel grinned with the same death's-head humor as before. "Bishop Trimer decided Hammer's Slammers weren't worth their price," Hammer said. "It wouldn't bother me if by the end of today, his Eminence had decided he was wrong on that."

Hammer touched a hidden switch and static flooded the screen.

"Four-six to Six," came Scratchard's voice, delayed until the laser link was broken. "We're ready, sir. Over."

"Four-six," Tyl said as he shrugged his armor loose over his sweating torso. "I'm on my way."

He left the laser communicator set up where it was. He'd need it again after the operation was over.

In the event that he survived.

CHAPTER TWENTY-SIX

"—gathered together at the dawn of a new age for our nation, our planet, and our God," said the voice.

Bishop Trimer's words had a touch of excitement remaining to them, despite being attenuated through multiple steps before they got to Tyl's helmet. Anne McGill aimed a directional microphone from the cathedral to the seafront altar, below her and over a kilometer away.

Trimer's speech was patched through the commo gear hidden between the woman's breasts, then shuttled by the UDB artificial intelligence over the inter-unit frequency to Tyl Koopman.

"We could shoot the bastard easy as listen to him," Scratchard said as he held out a shoulder weapon to his captain.

Only the two of them among the ninety-eight troopers in the rotunda had helmets that would receive the transmission. The other Slammers watched in silence as varied as their individual personalities: frightened; feral; cautious; and not a few with anticipation that drew back their lips in memory of past events. . . .

"Might break the back of the rebellion," Tyl said.

He had to will his eyes to focus on Scratchard's face, on anything as near as the walls of the big room. "Sure as blood that lot—" he touched his helmet over the tiny speaker "—they'd burn the city down to bricks 'n bare concrete. Might as well nuke 'em as that."

His voice didn't sound, even to him, as if he much cared. He wasn't sure he did care. He wasn't really involved with things that could be or might be . . . or even were.

"With dawn comes the light," the Bishop was saying. "With this dawn, the Lord brings us also the new light of freedom in the person of the man he has commanded me to anoint President of Bamberia."

"Jack, I don't need that," Tyl said peevishly. Sight of the 2 cm weapon being pushed toward him had brought him back to reality; irritation had succeeded where abstracts like survival and success could not. "I got a gun, remember?"

He slapped the receiver of the submachinegun under his arm, then noticed that the whole company was carrying double as well as being festooned with bandoliers and strings of grenades.

"UDB's weapons stores were here in the Palace," the sergeant major explained patiently. "Their el-tee, he told us go ahead. Sir, we don't got far t' go. And I swear, they all jam."

Scratchard grinned sadly. He lifted his right

boot to display the hilt of his fighting knife, though with his hands full he couldn't touch it for emphasis. "Even these, the blade can break. When you really don't want t' see that."

"Sorry," said Tyl, glad beyond words to be back in the present with sweaty palms and an itch between his shoulder blades that he couldn't have scratched even if it weren't covered by his clamshell armor.

"Blazes," he added as he checked the load—full magazine, chamber empty. "Here's my treatment a' choice anyhow. I'll take punch over pecka-pecka-pecka any day."

He looked up and glared around the circle of his troops as if seeing them for the first time. Pretty nearly he was. Good men, good soldiers; and just the team to pull the plug on Trimer and the bully-boys who thought they owned the streets when the Slammers were in town.

"Thomas Chastain has mounted the dais," said Anne McGill. She sounded calm, but the distance in her voice was more than an electronic artifact. "Both Chastain brothers. The faction heads are present, and so are several churchmen, standing beneath the crucifix."

Tyl keyed the command channel while ducking through the bandolier of 2 cm magazines the sergeant major held for him.

"Orange to Blue Six," he said, using the code he and the UDB officer had set up in a few seconds when they realized that they'd need it. "Report."

"Blue Six ready," said Desoix's voice.

"Orange to Blue Three. Report."

"Blue Three ready," said a voice Tyl didn't recognize, the non-com in charge of the Gun Three near the east entrance to the plaza.

"Orange Six to Blue," Tyl said. "We're moving into position . . . now."

He cut down with his right index finger. Before the gesture ended, Sergeant Kekkonan was leading the first squad into the incipient dawn over Bamberg City.

CHAPTER TWENTY-SEVEN

"I figured they'd a' burned it down, the way they was going last night," said Lachere, blinking around the warehouse from the driver's seat.

"Tonight," he said, correcting himself in mild wonder.

"Senter, what's the street look like?" Desoix asked from the gun saddle. Beneath him the calliope quivered like a sleeping hound, its being at placid idle—but ready to rend and bellow the instant it was aroused.

Desoix couldn't blame his subordinate for thinking more than a few hours had passed since they first entered this warehouse. It seemed like a lifetime—

And that wasn't a thought Lieutenant Charles Desoix wanted to pursue, even in the privacy of his own mind.

"I don't see anybody out, sir," the other clerk

called from the half-open pedestrian door. "Maybe lookin' out a window, I can't tell. But none a' the big mobs like when we got here."

Re-entering the warehouse without being caught up—or cut down—by the bands of bravos heading toward the plaza had been the trickiest part of the operation so far. Stealth was the only option open to Desoix and his two companions. Even if Koopman had been willing—been able, it didn't matter —to spare a squad in support, a firefight would still mean sure disaster for the plan as well as for the unit.

"All right, Senter," Desoix said. "Open the main doors and climb aboard."

Lachere was bringing the fans up to driving velocity without orders. He wasn't a great driver, but he'd handled air cushion vehicles before and could maneuver the calliope well enough for present needs.

The suction roar boomed in the cavernous room while Senter struggled with the unfamiliar door mechanism. The warehouse staff—manager, loaders, and guards—had disappeared at the first sign of trouble, leaving nothing behind but crated goods and the heavy effluvium of tobacco to be stirred into a frenzy by the calliope's drive fans.

The door rumbled upward; Senter scampered toward the gun vehicle. Desoix smiled. He'd been ready to clear their way with his eight 3 cm guns if necessary.

He had ordered control to lock the general frequency out of his headset. Captain Koopman was in charge of this operation, so Desoix didn't have to listen to the running commentary about what the mob in the plaza was doing.

If he listened on that frequency, he would hear

Anne; and he would have to remember where she was and how certainly she would die if he failed.

"Ready, sir?" Lachere demanded, shouting as though his voice weren't being transmitted over the intercom channel.

Desoix raised a hand in bar. "Blue Six to all Blue and Orange units," he said. "We're moving into position—now."

He chopped his hand.

Lachere accelerated them into the street with a clear view of the plaza's south stairhead, two blocks away.

Metal shrieked as Lachere side-swiped the door-jamb, but none of the calliope's scratch crew noticed the sound.

CHAPTER TWENTY-EIGHT

"I'm with you!" said Pedro Delcorio, gripping Tyl's shoulder from behind.

He was almost with the angels, because Tyl spun and punched the young noble in the belly with the weapon he'd just charged, his finger taking up slack.

"Careful, sonny," the Slammers officer said as intellect twitched away the gun that reflex had pointed.

Tyl felt light, as though his body were suspended on wires that someone else was holding. His skin was covered with a sheen of sweat that had nothing to do with the night's mild breezes.

Pedro wore a uniform—a service uniform, probably; though the clinking, glittering medals on both sides of the chest indicated that the kid still had something to learn about combat conditions. He also wore a determined expression and a pistol in a polished holster.

"You're doing this for my family," Pedro said. "One of us should be with you."

"That why we're doing it?" Tyl asked, marveling at the lilt in his own voice. Tyl wasn't sure the kid knew how close he'd come to dying a moment before. "Well, it'll do unless a better reason comes along. Stick close, boy, and leave that—" he nodded toward the gun "—in its holster."

He had a squad on the levee and a squad deployed to cover the boulevard and medians separating the Palace from the cathedral. The rest of the Slammers were moving at a nervous shuffle down the river drive—bunched more than he liked, than anybody'd like, but they were going to need all the firepower available to clear the mall in a hurry. Those hydraulic gates were the key to the operation: the key to bare safety, much less success.

No one seemed to be out, but Tyl could hear occasional shouts in the distance as well as the antiphonal roars from the plaza—though the latter were directed upward, into the sulphurous dawn, by the flood walls. Litter of all sorts splotched the pavement, waste and shattered valuables as well as a few bodies.

One of the crumpled bodies jumped up ahead of them. The drunk tottered backward when his foot slipped on the bottle which had put him there in the first place.

Tyl's point man fired a ten-shot burst—far too long—at the drunk. The bolts splashed all around the target, cyan flashes and the white blaze of lime burned out of the concrete. None of the rounds hit the intended victim.

A sergeant jumped to the shooter's side and slapped him hard on the helmet. "Cop-head!" he snarled. "Cop-head! Get your ass behind me. And if you shoot again without orders, you better have the muzzle in your mouth!"

The drunk scrambled in the general direction of the cathedral, stumbling and rolling on the ground to rise and stumble again. The air bit with the odors of ozone and quicklime.

The company shuffled onward with a squad leader in front.

"Blue Six to all Blue and Orange units," said Tyl's commo helmet. Desoix sounded tight, a message played ten percent faster than it'd been recorded. "We're moving into position—now."

The point man paused at the base of the ramp to the mall and the plaza's main stairs.

"Check your loads, boys," said Sergeant Major Scratchard over the unit push. Jack was back with the three squads of the second wave, but Tyl didn't expect him to stay there long when the shooting started.

"Sir," reported the point sergeant, using the command channel, "the gates are shut on this side."

"Orange Six to all Blue and Orange," Tyl ordered as he ran the ten meters to where the non-com paused. "Don't bloody move. We got a problem."

The gates separating the mall from the west river drive were as massive and invulnerable as those facing the plaza itself.

They were closed, just as the point man had said.

Tyl ran up the ramp, his bandoliers clashing against one another. The slung submachinegun gouged his hip beneath the flare of his armor. The gates were solid, solid enough to shrug away tidal surges with more power than a battery of artillery.

There was no way one company without demolition charges or heavy weapons was going to force its way through.

The small vitril windows in the gate panels were too scarred and dirty to show more than hinted movement, but there was a speaker plate in one of the pillars. Nothing ventured. . . .

Tyl keyed the speaker and said, "Open these gates at once, in the name of Bishop Trimer!"

The crowd in the plaza cheered deafeningly, shaking the earth like a distant bomb-blast.

Shadows, colors, shifted within the closed mall. The plate replied in the voice of Colonel Drescher, "Go away, little lap-dog. The Executive Guard is neutral, as I told you. And this is where we choose to exercise our neutrality."

The crowd thundered, working itself into blood-thirsty enthusiasm.

Tyl turned his back on the reinforced concrete and touched his commo helmet. His troops were crouching, watching him. Those who wore their shields down had saffron bubbles for faces, painted by the glow which preceded the sun.

"Orange to Blue Six," Tyl said. "We're screwed. The Guards 're holding the mall and they got it shut up. We can't get in, and if we tried we'd bring the whole bunch down on us. Save what you can, buddy. Over."

He'd forgotten that Anne McGill had access to the circuit. Before Desoix could speak, her voice rang like shards of crystal through Tyl's helmet, saying, "The river level has dropped. You can go under the plaza on a barge and come up beneath the altar."

The cross on the cathedral dome was beginning to blaze with sunlight. McGill's angle was on the seafront. She couldn't see any of the troops, Tyl's or the pair of calliopes, and she wouldn't have understood a *bloody* thing if she had been able to watch them. Bloody woman, bloody planet. . . .

Bloody fool, Captain Tyl Koopman, to be standing here. Nobody he saw was moving except Scratchard, clumping up the ramp to his captain's side. If Ripper Jack were bothered by his knees or the doubled load of weaponry, there was no sign of it on his expectant face.

"Tyl, she's right," Desoix was saying. "Most of the louvers are still closed, so there's no risk of drifting out to sea, but the maintenance catwalks lead straight up to the control house. The altar."

"Roger on the river level," the sergeant major muttered with his lips alone. He must've spoken to the non-com on the levee, using one of the support frequencies so as not to tie up the command push.

Tyl looked up at the sky, bright and clear after a night that was neither.

"Tyl, we'll give the support we can," Desoix said.

Both officers knew exactly what the change of plan would mean. They weren't going to be able to *talk* to the mob when they came up into the plaza. Desoix was apparently willing to go along with the change.

Wonder what the Colonel would say?

Colonel Hammer wasn't here. Tyl Koopman was, and he was ready to go along with it too. More fool him.

"Orange Six to all Orange personnel," he said on the unit push. "We're going to board the nearest barge and cut it loose so we drift to the dam at the other end of the plaza. . . ."

CHAPTER TWENTY-NINE

Some of the men were still scrambling aboard the barge, the second of the ten in line rather than the nearest, because it seemed less likely to scrape the whole distance along the concrete channel. Tyl didn't hear the order Jack Scratchard muttered into his commo helmet, but troopers standing by three of the four cables opened fire simultaneously.

Arm-thick ropes of woven steel parted in individual flashes. The barge sagged outward, its stern thumping the fenders of the vessel to port. Only the starboard bow line beside Tyl and the sergeant major held their barge against the current sucking them seaward.

The vertical lights on the walls, faintly green, merged as the channel drew outward toward the river's broad mouth and the dam closing it. They reflected from the water surface, now five meters

beneath the concrete roof—though it was still wet
enough to scatter the light back again in turn.

"Hold one, Jack," Tyl said as he remembered
there was another thing he needed to do before
they slipped beneath the plaza. He keyed his
helmet on the general inter-unit frequency and
said, "Orange Six to all Orange personnel. I am
ordering you to carry out an attack on the Bamberg
citizens assembled in the plaza. Anyone who re-
fuses to obey my order will be shot."

"Via!" cried one of the nearer soldiers. "*I'm* not
afraid to go, sir!"

"Shut up, you fool!" snarled Ripper Jack. "Don't
you understand? He's just covered your ass for
afterwards!"

Tyl grinned bleakly at the sergeant major. Everybody seemed to have boarded the vessel, cling-
ing to one another and balancing on the curves of
hogsheads. "Cut 'er loose," he said quietly.

Scratchard's powergun blasted the remaining cable with a blue-green glare and a gout of white
sparks whose trails lingered in the air as the barge
lurched forward.

Their stern brushed along the portside barge
until they drifted fully clear. The grind of metal
against the polymer fenders was unpleasant. Friction spun them slowly counterclockwise until they
swung free.

They continued to rotate for the full distance
beneath the widening channel. One trooper vom-
ited over his neighbor's backplate, though that
was more likely nerves than the gentle, gently
frustrating, motion.

Light coming through the louvered flood gates
was already brighter than the greenish artificial
sources on either wall. It was still diffuse sky-glow

rather than the glare of direct sun, but the timing was going to be very close.

The barge grounded broadside with a crash that knocked down anybody who was standing. Perhaps because of their rotation, they'd remained pretty well centered in the channel. Individually and without waiting for orders, the troopers nearest the catwalk jumped to it and began to lower a floating stage like the one on the dam's exterior.

"They must 've heard something," Tyl grumbled. The variety of metallic sounds the barge made echoed like a boiler works among the planes of water and concrete. But as soon as the barge had slipped its lines, Tyl had been unable to hear even a whisper of what he knew was a sky-shattering clamor from the crowded plaza. Probably those above were equally insulated.

And anyway, it didn't matter now. Tyl pressed forward to the pontoon-mounted stage and the stairs of steel grating leading up to the open hatch of the control room. Tyl's rank took him through his jostling men, but it was all he could do not to use his elbows and gun butt to force his way faster.

He had to remember that he was commanding a unit, not throwing his life away for no reason he could explain even to himself. He had to act as if there were military purpose to what he was about to do.

Only two men could stand abreast on the punched-steel stair treads, and that by pressing hard against the rails. The control room was almost as tight, space for ten men being filled by a dozen. Tyl squeezed his way in, pausing in the hatchway. When he turned to address his troops, he found the sergeant major just behind him.

It would have been nice to organize this better; but it would have been nicer yet for somebody else to be doing it. Or no one at all.

"Stop bloody pushing!" Tyl snapped on the unit frequency. Inside the control room, his signal would have been drunk by the meter-thick floor of the plaza. No wonder sound didn't get through.

Motion stopped, except for the gentle resilience of the barge's fenders against the closed flood-gates.

"There's one door out into the plaza," Tyl said simply. "We'll deploy through it, spread out as much as possible. If it doesn't work out, try to withdraw toward the east or west stairs, maybe the calliopes can give us some cover. Do your jobs, boys, and we'll come through this all right."

Scratchard laid a hand on the captain's elbow, then keyed his own helmet and said, "Listen up. This is nothin' you don't know. There's a lot of people up there."

He pumped the muzzle of his submachinegun toward the ceiling. "So long as there's one of 'em standing, none of us 're safe. Got that?"

Heads nodded, hands stroked the iridium barrels of powerguns. Some of the recruits exchanged glances.

"Then let's go," the sergeant major said simply. He hefted himself toward the hatchway.

Tyl blocked him. "I want you below, Jack," he said. "Last man out."

Scratchard grinned and shook his head. "I briefed Kekkonan for that," he said.

Tyl hesitated.

Scratchard's face sobered. "Cap'n," he said. "This don't take good knees. What it takes, I got."

"All right, let's go," said Tyl very softly. "But I'm the first through the door."

He pushed his way to the door out onto the plaza, hearing the sergeant major wheezing a step behind.

CHAPTER THIRTY

Anne McGill couldn't see the sun, but the edges of the House of Grace gleamed as they bent light from the orb already over the horizon to the northeast.

The crucifix on the seafront altar was golden and dazzling. The sun had not yet reached it, but Bishop Trimer was too good a showman not to allow for that: the gilt symbol was equipped with a surface-discharge system like that which made expensive clothing shimmer. What was good enough for the Consistory Room was good enough for God—as he was represented here in Bamberg City.

"Anne, what's happening in the plaza?" said the tiny phone in her left ear. "Do you see any sign of the, of Koopman? Over."

She was kneeling as if in an attitude of prayer, though she faced the half-open window. There were scores of others in the cathedral this morning, but no one would disturb another penitent. Like her, they were wrapped in their cloaks and their prayers.

And perhaps all of their prayers were as complex and uncertain as those of Anne McGill, lookout for a pair of mercenary companies and mistress of a man whom she had prevented from retreating with her to a place of safety.

"Oh Charles," she whispered. "Oh Charles."

Then she touched the control of her throat mike and said in a firm voice, "Chastain is kneeling before Bishop Trimer in front of the crucifix. He's putting a —I don't know, maybe the seal of office around his neck but I thought that was still in the Palace. . . ."

The finger-long directional microphone was clipped to the window transom which held it steady and unobtrusive. UDB stores included optical equipment as powerful and sophisticated as the audio pick-up; but in use, an electronic telescope looked like exactly what it was—military hardware, and a dead give-away of the person using it.

She had only her naked eyes. Though she squinted she couldn't be sure—

"The Slammers, curse it!" her lover's voice snapped in her ear. Charles' tongue suppressed the further words, "you idiot," but they were there in his tone. "Is there any sign of them?"

"No, no," she cried desperately. She'd forgotten to turn on her microphone. "Charles, no," she said with her thumb pressing the switch as if to crush it. "Chastain is rising and the crowd—"

Anne didn't see the door beneath the altar open the first time. There was only a flicker of movement in her peripheral vision, ajar and then closed.

Her subconscious was still trying to identify it when a dozen flashes lighted the front of the crowd facing the altar.

For another moment, she thought those were part of the celebration, but people were sprawling away from the flashes. A second later, the popping sound of the grenades going off reached her vantage point.

Men were spilling out of the altar building. The bolts from their weapons hurt Anne's eyes, even shielded by distance and full dawn.

"Charles!" she cried, careless now of who might hear her in the gallery. "It's started! They're—"

The air near the seafront echoed with a crashing hiss like that of a dragon striking. Anne McGill had never heard anything like it before. She didn't know that it was a calliope firing—but she knew that it meant death.

Buildings hid her view of the impact zone at the west stairhead of the plaza, but some of the debris flung a hundred meters in the air could still be identified as parts of human bodies.

CHAPTER FOURTEEN

CHAPTER THIRTY-ONE

When the grenades burst, Scratchard jerked the metal door open again—a milli-second before a slow fuse detonated the last of their greeting cards. A scrap of glass-fiber shrapnel drew a line across the back of Tyl's left thumb.

He didn't notice it. He was already shooting from the hip at the first person he saw as he swung through the doorway, a baton-waving orderly whose face was almost as white as his robe except where blood spattered both of them.

Tyl's target was a meter and a half away from his gun muzzle. He missed. The red cape and shoulder of a woman beside the orderly exploded in a cyan flash.

The orderly swung his baton in desperation, but he was already dead. Jack Scratchard put a burst into his face before pointing his submachinegun at the group on the altar above and behind them. Trimer flattened, carrrying Thom Chastain with him, but blue-green fire flicked the chests of both gang bosses.

Tyl hadn't appreciated the noise. It beat on him, a pressure squeezing him into his armor and engulfing the usual *thump!* of his bolts heating the air like miniature lightning. He butted his weapon firmly against his shoulder and fired three times to clear the area to his right.

The targets fell. Their eyes were still startled and blinking, though the 2 cm bolts had scooped their chests into fire and a sludge of gore.

Tyl strode onward, making room for the troopers behind him as he'd planned, as he'd ordered in some distant other universe.

An army officer leaped from the altar with a pistol in his hand, either seeking shelter in the crowd or fleeing Scratchard's quick gun in blind panic. The Bamberg soldier doubled up as fate carried him past Tyl's muzzle and reflex squeezed the powergun's trigger.

Short range but a nice crossing shot. Tyl was fine and the noise, the shouting, was better protection than his helmet and clamshell. But there were too many of the bastards, a mass like the sea itself, and Tyl was all alone in a tide that would wash over him and his men no matter what they—

One calliope, then the other, opened fire. Not even crowd noise and the adrenalin coursing through his blood could keep the Slammers officer from noticing that.

He stepped forward, his right shoulder against the altar building to keep him from slipping. Each shot was aimed, and none of them missed.

In a manner of speaking, Tyl Koopman's face wore a smile.

CHAPTER THIRTY-TWO

The bollards at the stairhead were hidden by the units on guard, thugs wearing the colors of both factions and a detachment of hospital orderlies. There were at least fifty heavily-armed men and women in plain sight of Desoix's calliope—and it was only a matter of moments before one of them would turn from the ceremony and look up the street.

There weren't many options available then.

"Is there any sign of them?" Desoix shouted to—at—his mistress as she nattered on about what Trimer was using as he swore in his stooge as President.

Lachere was twisted around in the driver's saddle, peering back at his lieutenant and chewing the end of a cold cigar, a habit he'd picked up in the months they'd been stationed here. He didn't look worried, but Senter had enough fear in his expression for both clerks as he stared at Desoix's profile from his station at the loading console.

"Charles!" cried the voice he had let through to him again for necessity. "It's—"

Desoix had already heard the muffled exclamation points of the grenades.

"Blue Six to Blue Three," he said, manually cutting away to the unit frequency. "Open fire."

As his mouth voiced the final flat syllable, his right foot rocked forward on the firing pedal. Traversing left to right, Desoix swept the stairhead clear of all obstructions with the eight ravening barrels of his calliope.

The big weapon was intended for computer-directed air defense. Under manual control, its sights were only a little more sophisticated than those of shoulder-fired powerguns: a hologrammatic sight picture with a bead in the center to mark the point of impact.

Nothing more was required.

Several of the guards turned when the grenades went off, instinctively looking for escape and instead seeing behind them the calliope's lowered muzzles. One of the orderlies got off a burst with his submachinegun.

The bullets missed by a hundred meters in the two blocks they were meant to travel. Concrete, steel, and flesh—most particularly flesh—vaporized as the calliope chewed across the stairhead in a three-second burst.

Desoix switched to intercom with the hand he didn't need for the moment on the elevation control and said, "Lachere, advance toward the stairhead at a—"

Faces appeared around the seawall just north of where the bollards had been before the gun burned them away. The high-intensity 3 cm ammunition had shattered concrete at the start of the burst before Desoix traversed away. His right hand rolled forward on the twist-grip, reversing the direction in which the barrel array rotated on its gimbals.

More of the wall disintegrated in cyan light and the white glare of lime burned free of the concrete by enormously concentrated energy. Most of the rioters had time to duck back behind the wall before the second burst raked it.

The wall didn't save them. Multiple impacts tore it apart and then flash-heated the water in their own bodies into steam explosions.

Beneath Desoix, the skirts of the calliope's plenum chamber dragged the pavement. Air had enough mass to recoil when it was heated to a plasma and expelled from the eight tubes as the gun fired. Lachere drove forward, correcting inexpertly against the calliope's pitch and yaw.

Gunfire was a blue-green shield against the roar from the plaza, but in the moments between bursts the mob's voice asserted itself over the numbness of ringing breech-blocks and slamming air. The stairhead was now within a hundred meters as the gun drove onward. There was a haze over the target area—steam and dust, burnt lime and burning bodies.

Desoix's faceshield protected him from the sun-hot flash of his guns. Events, thundering forward as implacably as an avalanche, shielded him from awareness that would have been as devastating to him as being blinded.

With no target but the roiling haze, Desoix triggered another burst when they were ten meters from the stairhead. Fragments blown clear by the impacts proved that there had been people sheltering beneath eye level but accessible to the upper pair of gun tubes.

"Sir?" a voice demanded, Lachere slowing and ready to ground the vehicle before they lurched over the scars where the bollards had been and their bow tilted down the steps.

"Go!" Desoix shouted, knowing that the plenum chamber would spill its air in the angle of the stair treads and that their unaided fans would never be able to lift the calliope away once they had committed.

Koopman and his company of Slammers weren't going anywhere either, unless they all succeeded in the most certain and irrevocable way possible.

The stench of ozone and ruin boiled out from beneath the drive fans an instant before the calliope rocked forward. Gravity aided its motion for an instant before the friction of steel against stone grounded the skirts. The plaza was a sea of faces with a roar like the surf.

Bullets rang off the hull and splashed the glowing iridium of one port-side barrel. The doors of the mall at the head of the main stairs were open toward the plaza. Men there were firing assault rifles at the calliope. Some of them were either good or very lucky.

Desoix rotated his gun carriage.

"Sir!" Senter cried with his helmet against the lieutenant's. "Those aren't the mob! They're the Guard!"

"Feed your guns, soldier!" said Charles Desoix. The open flood gates filled his sight hologram.

He rocked the firing pedal down and began to traverse his target in a blaze of light.

CHAPTER THIRTY-THREE

Tyl's index finger tightened. The gunstock pummeled his shoulder. The center of his faceshield went momentarily black as it mirrored away the flash that would otherwise have blinded him.

A finger of plastic flipped up into his sight picture, indicating that he'd just fired the last charge in his weapon. He reached for another magazine.

A hospital orderly stopped trying to claw through the mass of other panicked humans and turned to face Tyl. He was less than ten meters away and held a pistol.

Tyl raised the tube of 2 cm ammunition to the loading gate in the forestock and burned the nail and third knuckle of all the fingers on his left hand. He'd already put several magazines through the powergun, so its barrel was white hot.

He dropped the magazine. The orderly shot him in the center of the chest.

There was no sound any more in the plaza. Tyl could see everything down to the last hair on the moustache of the orderly collapsing around a bolt from somebody else's powergun. His armor spread the bullet's impact, but it felt as if they'd driven a tank over his chest. Maybe if he didn't move. . . .

The calliope which was canted down the west staircase opened fire again.

Only three of the eight barrels were live at the moment. Individual bolts made a thump as ionized air ripped from the barrel; they crossed the plaza a few meters over Tyl's head as a microsecond *hiss*! and a flash of light so saturated that it seemed palpable.

Everything the bolts hit was disintegrated with a crash sharper than a bomb going off, solids converted to gas and plasma as suddenly as the light-swift bursts of energy had snapped through the air. The plaza's concrete flooring gouted in explosions of dazzling white—

But the crowd was packed too thickly for that to happen often. The calliope's angle allowed its crew to rake the mob from above. Each 3 cm bolt hit like the hoof of a horse galloping over soft ground, hurling spray and bits of the footing in every direction before lifting to hammer the surface again.

Bodies crumpled in windrows. Screaming rioters climbed the fallen on their way toward the main stairs, already packed with their fellows.

The guns continued to fire.

"If I can hear, I can move," Tyl said, mouthing the words because that *was* his first movement since the bullet hit him.

He knelt to pick up the magazine he had dropped. The pain that flooded him, hot needles being jabbed into his whole chest, made him drop the empty gun instead.

He couldn't breathe. He didn't fall down because his muscles were locked in a web of flesh surrounding a center of pulsing red agony.

The spasm passed.

Tyl's troopers were spread in a ragged semicircle, centering on the building from which they'd deployed. He was near the east stairs; the treads were covered with bodies.

Rebels had been shot in the back as they tried to run from the soldiers and the blue-green scintillance of hand weapons. If they reached the top of the stairs, Gun Three on the seafront hurled them back as a puree and a scattering of fragments.

The west stairs were relatively empty, because the mob had time to clear it in the face of the calliope staggering toward them. They died on the plaza floor, because they'd run toward the debouching infantry; but the steps gleamed white in the sunlight and provided a pure contrast to the bodies and garments crumpled everywhere else in muddy profusion.

Tyl left the 2 cm weapon where he'd dropped it; he raised his submachinegun. It felt light by contrast with the thick iridium barrel of the shoulder weapon, but he still had trouble aiming.

It was hot, and Tyl was as thirsty as he ever remembered being. Ozone had lifted all the mucus away from the membranes of his nose and throat. The mordant gas was concentrated by shooting in the enclosed wedge of the plaza. The skin of Tyl's face and hands prickled as if sunburned.

He aimed at a face and missed high, the barrel wobbling, sending the round into the back of somebody a hundred meters away on the main stairs.

He lowered the muzzle and fired again, fired again, fired again.

Single shots, aimed at anyone who looked toward him instead of trying to get away. Second choice for targets were the white robes of orderlies, most of whom had been armed—though few enough had the discipline to stand in chaos against the mercenaries' armor and overwhelming firepower.

Third choice was whoever filled the sight picture next. None of the mercenaries were safe so long as one of the others was standing.

The calliope opened up again. Desoix had unjammed or reloaded six of the barrels. A thick line staggered through the mob like the track of a tornado across a corn field.

Tyl fired; fired again; fired again. . . .

CHAPTER THIRTY-FOUR

It was very quiet.

Desoix watched the men from Gun Three's doubled crew as they picked their way across the plaza at his orders. Sergeant Blaney was leading the quartet himself. They were carrying their submachineguns ready and moving with a gingerly awkwardness, trying to avoid stepping in the carnage.

Nobody could get down the east stairs without smearing his boots to the ankles with blood.

"They could hurry up with the water," Lachere muttered.

"They didn't see it happen," Desoix said. He lay across the firing console, his chin on his hands and his elbows on the control grips he no longer needed to twist.

He closed his eyes for a moment instead of rubbing them.

Desoix's hands and face, like those of his men, were black with iridium burned from the calliope's bores by the continuous firing. The vapor had condensed in the air and settled as dust over everything within ten meters of the muzzles. Rubbing his eyes before he washed would drive the finely-divided metal under the lids, into the orbits.

Desoix kept reminding himself that it would matter to him some day, when he wasn't so tired.

"They just shot when somebody ran up the stairs and gave them a target," he continued in the croak that was all the voice remaining to him until Blaney arrived with the water. "It wasn't like—"

He wanted to raise his arm to indicate the plaza's carpet of the dead, but waggling an index finger was as much as he had need or energy to accomplish. "It wasn't what we had, all targets, and it. . . ."

Desoix tried to remember how he would have felt if he had come upon this scene an hour earlier. He couldn't, so he let his voice trail off.

A lot of them must have gotten out when somebody opened the gates at either end of the mall. Desoix had tried to avoid raking the mall and the main stairs. The mercenaries had to end the insurrection and clear the plaza for their own safety, but the civilians swept out by fear were as harmless as their fellows who filled the sight picture as the calliope coughed and traversed.

There'd been just the one long burst which cleared the mall of riflemen.

Cleared it of life.

"Here you go, sir," said Blaney, skipping up the last few steps with a four-liter canteen and hopping onto the deck of the calliope.

"Took yer bloody time," Lachere repeated as he snatched the canteen another of the newcomers offered him. He began slurping the water down so greedily that he choked and sprayed a mouthful out his nostrils.

Senter was drinking also. He hunched down behind the breeches of the guns he had been feeding, so that he could not see any of what surrounded the calliope. Even so, the clerk's eyelids were pressed tightly together except for brief flashes that showed his dilated pupils.

"Ah, where's Major Borodin, sir?" Blaney asked.

Desoix closed his eyes again, luxuriating in the feel of warm water swirling in his mouth.

Gun Three had full supplies for its double crew before the shooting started. Desoix hadn't thought to load himself and his two clerks with water before they set out.

He hadn't been planning; just reacting, stimulus by stimulus, to a situation over which he had abdicated conscious control.

"The Major's back at the Palace," Desoix said. "President Delcorio told me he wanted a trustworthy officer with him, so I commanded the field operations myself."

He didn't care about himself any more. He stuck to the story he had arranged with Delcorio because it was as easy to tell as the truth . . . and because Desoix still felt a rush of loyalty to his battery commander.

They'd succeeded, and Major Borodin could have his portion of the triumph if he wanted it.

Charles Desoix wished it had been him, not Borodin, who had spent the last two hours locked in a storeroom in the Palace. But his memory would not permit him to think that, even as a fantasy.

"Blaney," he said aloud. "I'm putting you in command of this gun until we get straightened around. I'm going down to check with Captain Koopman." He nodded toward the cluster of gray and khaki soldiers sprawled near the altar.

"Ah, sir?" Blaney said in a nervous tone.

Desoix paused after swinging his leg over the gunner's saddle. He shrugged, as much response as he felt like making at the moment.

"Sir, we started taking sniper fire, had two guys hurt," Blaney went on. "We—I laid the gun on the hospital, put a burst into it to, you know, get their attention. Ah, the sniping stopped."

"Via, you really did, didn't you?" said the officer, amazed that he hadn't noticed the damage before.

Gun Three had a flat angle on the south face of the glittering building. Almost a third of the vitril panels on that side were gone in a raking slash from the ground floor to the twentieth. The bolts wouldn't have penetrated the hospital, though the Lord knew what bits of the shattered windows had done when they flew around inside.

Charles Desoix began to laugh. He choked and had to grip the calliope's chassis in order to keep from falling over. He hadn't been sure that he would ever laugh again.

"Sergeant," he said, shutting his eyes because Blaney's stricken face would set him off again if he watched it. "You're afraid you're in trouble because of *that*?"

He risked a look at Blaney. The sergeant was nodding blankly.

Desoix gripped his subordinate's hand. "Don't

worry," he said. "Don't. I'll just tell them to put it on my account."

He took the canteen with him as he walked down the stairs toward Tyl Koopman. Halfway down, he stumbled when he slipped on a dismembered leg.

That set him laughing again.

CHAPTER THIRTY-FIVE

"Got twelve could use help," said the sergeant major as Tyl shuddered under the jets of topical anesthetic he was spraying onto his own chest.

Scratchard frowned and added, "Maybe you too, hey?"

"Via, I'm fine," Tyl said, trying to smooth the grimace that wanted to twist his face awry. "No dead?"

He looked around sharply and immediately wished he hadn't tried to move quite that fast.

Tyl's ceramic breastplate had stopped the bullet and spread its impact across the whole inner surface of the armor. That was survivable; but now, with the armor and his tunic stripped off, Tyl's chest was a symphony of bruising. His ribs and the seams of his tunic pockets were emphasized in purple, and the flesh between those highlights was a dull yellow-gray of its own.

Scratchard shrugged. "Krasinski took one in the face," he said. "Had 'er shield down too, but when your number's up. . . ."

Tyl sprayed anesthetic. The curse that ripped out of his mouth could have been directed at the way the mist settled across him and made the bruised flesh pucker as it chilled.

"Timmons stood on a grenade," Scratchard continued, squatting beside his captain. "Prob'ly his own. Told 'em not to screw with grenades after we committed, but they never listen, not when it gets. . ."

Scratchard's fingers were working with the gun he now carried, a slug-firing machine pistol. The magazine lay on the ground beside him. The trigger group came out, then the barrel tilted from the receiver at the touch of the sergeant major's experienced fingers.

Jack wasn't watching his hands. His eyes were open and empty, focused on the main stairs because there were no fallen troopers there.

They'd been his men too.

"One a' the recruits," Scratchard continued quietly, "he didn't want to go up the ladder."

Tyl looked at the non-com.

Scratchard shrugged again. "Kekkonan shot him. Wasn't a lotta time to discuss things."

"Kekkonan due another stripe?" Tyl asked.

"After this?" Scratchard replied, his voice bright with unexpected emotion. "We're *all* due bloody something, sir!"

His face blanked. His fingers began to reassemble the gun he'd picked up when he'd fired all the ammunition for both the powerguns he carried.

Tyl looked at their prisoners, the half dozen men who'd survived when Jack sprayed the group on the altar. Now they clustered near the low building, under the guns of a pair of troopers who'd been told to guard them.

The soldiers were too tired to pay much attention. The prisoners were too frightened to need guarding at all.

Thom Chastain still wore a gold-trimmed scarlet robe. A soldier had ripped away the chain and pendant Tyl remembered vaguely from earlier in the morning. Thom smiled like a porcelain doll, a hideous contrast with the tears which continued to shiver down his cheeks.

The tears were particularly noticeable because one of the gang bosses beside Thom on the altar had been shot in the neck. He'd been very active in his dying, painting everyone nearby with streaks of bright, oxygen-rich blood. The boy's tears washed tracks in the blood.

Bishop Trimer and three lesser priests stood a meter from the Chastains—and as far apart as turned backs and icy expressions could make them.

Father Laughlin was trying to hunch himself down to the height of other men. His white robes dragged the ground when he forgot to draw them up with his hands; their hem was bloody.

The prisoners weren't willing to sit down the way the Slammers did. But *nobody* was used to a scene like this.

"I never saw so many bodies," said Charles Desoix.

"Yeah, me too," Tyl agreed.

He hadn't seen the UDB officer walk up beside him. His eyes itched. He supposed there was something wrong with his peripheral vision from the ozone or the actinics—despite his faceshield.

"Water?" Desoix offered.

"Thanks," Tyl said, accepting the offer though water still sloshed in the canteen on his own belt. He drank and paused, then sipped again.

Where the calliope had raked the mob, corpses lay in rows like flotsam thrown onto the strand by a storm. Otherwise, the half of the plaza nearer the sea-front was strewn rather than carpeted with bodies. You could walk that far and, if you were careful, step only on concrete.

Bloody concrete.

Where the plaza narrowed toward the main stairs, there was no longer room even for the corpses. They were piled one upon another . . . five in a stack . . . a ramp ten meters deep, rising at the same angle as the stairs and composed of human flesh compressed by the weight of more humans— each trying to escape by clambering over his fellows, each dying in turn as the guns continued to fire.

The stench of scattered viscera was a sour miasma as the sun began to warm the plaza.

"How many, d'ye guess?" Tyl asked as he handed back the canteen.

He was sure his voice was normal, but he felt his body begin to shiver uncontrollably. It was the drugs, it *had* to be the anesthetic.

"Twenty thousand, thirty thousand," Desoix said. He cleared his throat, but his voice broke anyway as he tried to say, "They did, they. . ."

Desoix bent his head. When he lifted it again, he said in a voice as clear as the glitter of tears in his eyes, "I think as many were crushed trying to get away as we killed ourselves. But we killed enough."

Something moved at the head of the main stairs. Tyl aimed the submachinegun he'd picked up when he stood. Pain filled his torso like the fracture lines in breaking glass, but he didn't shudder any more. The sight picture was razor sharp.

An air car with the gold and crystal markings of the Palace slid through the mall and cruised down the main stairs. The vehicle was being driven low and slow, just above the surface, because surprising the troops here meant sudden death.

Even laymen could see that.

Tyl lowered his weapon, wondering what would have happened if he'd taken up the last trigger pressure and spilled John and Eunice Delcorio onto the bodies of so many of their opponents.

The car's driver and the man beside him were Palace servants, both in their sixties. They looked out of place, even without the pistols in issue holsters belted over their blue livery.

Major Borodin and Colonel Drescher rode in the middle pair of seats, ahead of the presidential couple.

The battery commander was the first to get out when the car grounded beside the mercenary officers. The electronic piping of Borodin's uniform glittered brighter than sunlight on the metal around him. He blinked at his surroundings, at the prisoners. Then he nodded to Desoix and said, "Lieutenant, you've, ah—carried out your orders in a satisfactory fashion."

Desoix saluted. "Thank you, sir," he said in a voice as dead as the stench of thirty thousand bodies.

Colonel Drescher followed Borodin, moving like a marionette with a broken wire. The flap of his holster was closed, but there was no gun inside. One of the Guard commander's polished boots was missing. He held the sole of the bare foot slightly above the concrete, where it would have been if he were fully dressed.

President Delcorio stepped from the vehicle and handed out his wife as if they were at a public function. Both of them were wearing cloth of gold, dazzling even though the car's fans had flung up bits of the carnage as it carried them through the plaza.

"Gentlemen," Delcorio said, nodding to Tyl and Desoix. His throat hadn't been wracked by the residues of battle, so his voice sounded subtly wrong in its smooth normalcy.

Pedro Delcorio was walking to join his uncle from the control room beneath the altar. He carried a pistol in his right hand. The bore of the powergun was bright and not scarred by use.

The President and his wife approached the prisoners. Major Borodin fluffed the thighs of his uniform; Drescher stood on one foot, his eyes looking out over the channel.

President Delcorio stared at the Bishop. The other priests hunched away, as if Delcorio's gaze were wind-blown sleet.

Trimer faced him squarely. The Bishop was a short man and slightly built even in the bulk of his episcopal garments, but he was very much alive. Looking at him, Tyl remembered the faint glow that firelight had washed across the eyes of Trimer's face carven on the House of Grace.

"Bishop," said John Delcorio. "I'm so glad my men were able to rescue you from this—" his foot delicately gestured toward the nearest body, a woman undressed by the grenade blast that killed her "—rabble."

Father Laughlin straightened so abruptly that he almost fell when he kicked the pile of communications and data-transfer equipment which his two fellows had piled on the ground. No one had bothered to strip the priests of their hardware, but they had done so themselves as quickly as they were able.

Perhaps the priests felt they could distance themselves from what had gone before . . . or what they expected to come later.

"Pres . . ." said Bishop Trimer cautiously. His voice was oil-smooth—until it cracked. "President?"

"Yes, very glad," Delcorio continued. "I think it must be that the Christ-denying elements were behind the riot. I'm sure they took you prisoner when they heard you had offered all the assets of the Church to support our crusade."

Laughlin threw his hands to his face, covering his mouth and a look of horror.

"Yes, all Church personalty," said Trimer. "Except what is needed for the immediate sustenance of the Lord's servants."

"All assets, real and personal, is what I'd heard," said the President. His voice was flat. The index finger of his right hand was rising as if to make a gesture, a cutting motion.

"Yes, personal property and all the estates of the Church outside of Bamberg City itself," said Bishop Trimer. He thrust out his chin, looking even more like the bas relief on the shot-scarred hospital.

Delcorio paused, then nodded. "Yes," he said. "That's what I understood. We'll go back to—"

Eunice Delcorio looked at Tyl. "You," she said in a clear voice, ignoring her husband and seemingly ignoring the fact that he had spoken. "Shoot these two."

She pointed toward the Chastains.

Tyl raised his submachinegun's muzzle skyward and stepped toward the President's wife.

"Sir!" shouted Ripper Jack Scratchard, close enough that his big hand gripped Tyl's shoulder. "Don't!"

Tyl pulled free. He took Eunice's right hand in his left and pressed her palm against the grip of the submachinegun. He forced her fingers closed. "Here," he said. "You do it."

He hadn't thought he was shouting, but he must have been from the way all of them stared at him, their faces growing pale.

He spun Eunice around to face the ramp of bodies. She was a solid woman and tried to resist, but that was nothing to him now. "It's easy," he said. "See how bloody easy it is?

"Do you *see*?"

A shot cracked. He *had* been shouting. The muzzle blast didn't seem loud at all.

Tyl turned. Scratchard fired his captured weapon again. Richie Chastain screamed and stumbed across his twin; Thom was already down with a hole behind his right ear and a line of blood from the corner of his mouth.

Scratchard fired twice more as the boy thrashed on his belly. The second bullet punched through the chest cavity and ricocheted from the ground with a hum of fury.

Tyl threw his gun down. He turned and tried to walk away, but he couldn't see anything. He would have fallen except that Scratchard took one of his arms and Desoix the other, holding him and standing between him and the Delcorios.

"Bishop Trimer," he heard the President saying. "Will you adjourn with us, please, to the Palace." There was no question in the tone. "We have some details to work out, and I think we'll be more comfortable there, though my servant situation is a—"

Tyl turned.

"Wait," he said. Everyone was watching him. There was a red blotch on the back of Eunice's hand where he'd held her, but he was as controlled as the tide, now. "I want doctors for my men."

He lifted his hand toward the House of Grace, glorying in the pain of moving. "You got a whole hospital, there. I want doctors, *now*, and I want every one of my boys treated like he was Christ himself. Understood?"

"Of course, of course," said Father Laughlin in the voice Tyl remembered from the Consistory Meeting.

The big priest turned to the man who had been wearing the commo set and snarled, "Well, get *on* it, Ryan. You heard the man!"

Ryan knelt and began speaking into the handset, glancing sometimes up at the hospital's shattered facade and sometimes back at the Slammers captain. The only color on the priest's face was a splotch of someone else's blood.

Trimer walked to the air car, arm in arm with President Delcorio.

Borodin and Drescher had already boarded. Neither of them would let their eyes focus on anything around them. When Pedro Delcorio squeezed in between them, the two officers made room without comment.

Father Laughlin would have followed the Bishop, but Eunice Delcorio glanced at his heavy form and gestured dismissingly. Laughlin watched the car lift into a hover; then, sinking his head low, he strode in the direction of the east stairs.

Tyl Koopman stood between his sergeant major and the UDB lieutenant. He was beginning to shiver again.

"What's it mean, d'ye suppose?" he whispered in the direction of the main stairs.

"Mean?" said Charles Desoix dispassionately. "It means that John Delcorio is President—President in more than name—for the first time. It means that he really has the resources to prosecute his crusade, the war on Two, to a successful conclusion. I doubt that would have been possible without the financial support of the Church."

"But who *cares*!" Tyl shouted. "D'ye mean we've got jobs for the next two years? Who bloody cares? Somebody'd 've hired us, you know that!"

"It means," said Jack Scratchard, "that we're alive and they're dead. That's all it means, sir."

"It's *got* to mean more than that," Tyl whispered.

But as he looked at the heaps and rows of bodies, tens of thousands of dead human beings stiffening in the sun, he couldn't put any real belief into the words.

CHAPTER THIRTY-SIX

The Slammers were gone.

Ambulances had carried their wounded off, each with a guard of other troopers ready to add a few more bodies to the day's bag if any of Trimer's men seemed less than perfectly dedicated to healing the wounded. Desoix thought he'd heard the sergeant major say something about bivouacking in the House of Grace, but he hadn't been paying much attention.

There was nothing here for him. He ought to leave himself.

Desoix turned. Anne McGill was walking toward him. She had thrown off the cloak that covered her in the cathedral and was wearing only a dress of white chiffon like the one in which she had greeted him the day before.

Her face was set. She was moving very slowly,

because she would not look down and her feet kept brushing the things that she refused to see.

Desoix began to tremble. He had unlatched his body armor, but he still had it on. The halves rattled against one another as he watched the woman approach.

There was nothing there. There couldn't be anything left there now.

It didn't matter. That was only one of many things which had died this morning. No doubt he'd feel it was an unimportant one in later years.

Anne put her arms around him, crushing her cheek against his though he was black with iridium dust and dried blood. "I'm so sorry," she whispered. "Charles, I—we. . . . Charles, I love you."

As if love could matter now.

Desoix put his arms around her, squeezing gently so that the edges of his armor would not bite into her soft flesh.

Love mattered, even now.

Afterword to Counting the Cost

HOW THEY GOT THAT WAY

I gained my first real insight into tanks when I was about eight years old and the local newspaper ran a picture of one, an M41 Walker Bulldog, on the front page.

The M41 isn't especially big. It's longer than the Studebaker my family had at the time but still a couple feet shorter than the 1960 Plymouth we owned later. At nine feet high and eleven feet wide, the tank was impressive but not really out of automotive scale.

What was striking about it was the way it had flattened a parked car when the tank's driver goofed during a Christmas Parade in Chicago. That picture proved to me that the power and lethality of a tank are out of all proportion to the size of the package.

*   *   *

I learned a lot more about tanks in 1970 when I was assigned to the 11th Armored Cavalry Regiment in Viet Nam.

Normally, interrogators like me were in slots at brigade level or higher. The Eleventh Cav was unusual in that each of its three squadrons in the field had a Battalion Intelligence Collection Center —pronounced like the pen—of four to six men. After a week or two at the rear echelon headquarters of my unit, I requested assignment to a BICC. A few weeks later, I joined Second Squadron in Cambodia.

Our BICC had a variety of personal and official gear—the tent was our largest item—which fitted into a trailer about the size of a middling-big U-Haul-It. We didn't have a *vehicle* of our own. When the squadron moved (as it generally did every week or two), the trailer was towed by one of the Headquarters Troop tracks; and we, the personnel, were split up as crew among the fighting vehicles.

The tanks were M48s, already obsolescent because the 90 mm main gun couldn't be trusted to penetrate the armor of new Soviet tanks. That wasn't a problem for us, since most of the opposition wore black pajamas and sandals cut from tire treads.

M48s have a normal complement of four men, but that was exceptionally high in the field. In one case, I rode as loader on a tank which would have been down to two men—driver and commander— without me. The Eleventh Cav was at almost double its official (Table of Organization) strength, but the excess personnel didn't trickle far enough from headquarters to reach the folks who were expected to do the actual fighting.

* * *

While I was there, a squadron in the field operated as four linked entities. Squadron headquarters (including the BICC) was a firebase, so called because the encampment included a battery of self-propelled 155 mm howitzers—six guns if none were deadlined.

Besides How Battery, the firebase included Headquarters Troop with half a dozen Armored Cavalry Assault Vehicles—ACAVs. These were simply M113 armored personnel carriers modified at the factory into combat vehicles. Each had a little steel cupola around a fifty caliber machinegun and a pintle-mounted M60 machinegun (7.62 mm) on either flank.

There were also a great number of other vehicles at the firebase: armored personnel carriers modified into trucks, high-sided command vehicles, and mobile flamethrowers (Zippos); maintenance vehicles with cranes to lift out and replace engines in the field; and a platoon of combat engineers with a modified M48 tank as well as the bulldozers that turned up an earthen berm around the whole site.

Apart from these headquarters units, the squadron was made up of a company of (nominally) seventeen M48 tanks; and three line troops with twelve ACAVs and six Sheridans apiece. The Sheridan is a deathtrap with a steel turret, an aluminum hull, and a 152 mm cannon whose ammunition generally caught fire if the vehicle hit a forty pound mine.

Either a line troop or the tank company laagered at the firebase at night for security. The other three formed separate night defensive positions within fire support range of How Battery.

I talked with a lot of people in the field, and I got a good first-hand look at the way an armored regiment conducts combat operations.

*   *   *

When I got back to the World, I resumed my hobby of writing fantasies. I'd sold three stories to August Derleth in the past; now I sold him a fourth, set in the late Roman Empire. Mr. Derleth paid for that story the day before he died.

With him gone, there was no market for what I was writing: short stories in the heroic fantasy subgenre. I kept writing them anyway, becoming more and more frustrated that they didn't sell. (I wasn't real tightly wrapped back then. It was a while before I realized just how screwy I was.)

Fortunately, writer-friends in Chapel Hill, Manly Wade Wellman and Karl Edward Wagner, suggested that I use Viet Nam as a setting. I tried it with immediate success, selling a horror fantasy to F&SF and a science fiction story to ANALOG.

I still had a professional problem. There were very few stories that someone with my limited skills could tell which were SF or fantasy, *and* which directly involved the Eleventh Cav. I decided to get around the issue by telling a story that was SF because the characters used ray guns instad of M16s . . . but was otherwise true, the way it had been described to me by the men who'd been there.

The story was THE BUTCHER'S BILL, and for it I created a mercenary armored regiment called Hammer's Slammers.

The hardware was easy. I'd spent enough time around combat vehicles to have a notion of their strengths and weaknesses. Hammer's vehicles were designed around the M48s and ACAVs I'd ridden, with some of the most glaring faults eliminated.

All the vehicles in the field with the Eleventh Cav were track-laying; that is, they had caterpillar treads instead of wheels. This was necessary because we never encamped on surfaced roads. Part of any move, even for headquarters units, was across stretches of jungle cleared minutes before by bulldozers fitted with Rome Plow blades.

The interior of a firebase was also bulldozed clear. Rain turned the bare soil either gooey or the consistency of wet soap. In both cases, it was impassable for wheeled vehicles. Our daily supplies came in by helicopter.

Tracks were absolutely necessary; and they were an absolute curse for the crewmen who had to maintain them.

Jungle soils dry to a coarse, gritty stone that abrades the tracks as they churn it up. When tracks wear, they loosen the way a bicycle chain does. To steer a tracked vehicle, you brake one tread while the other continues to turn. If the tracks are severely worn, you're certain to throw one.

If they're not worn, you may throw one anyway.

Replacing a track in the field means the crew has to break the loop; drive off it with the road wheels and the good track while another vehicle stretches the broken track; reverse onto the straightened track, hand-feeding the free end up over the drive sprocket and along the return rollers; and then mate the ends into a loop again.

You may very well throw the same track ten minutes later.

Because of that problem (and suspension problems. Want to guess how long torsion bars last on a fifty ton tank bouncing over rough terrain?) I decided my supertanks had to be air cushion vehicles. That would be practical only if fuel supply weren't a problem, so that the fans could be powerful enough to keep the huge mass stable even though it didn't touch the ground.

I'm a writer, not an engineer. I didn't have any difficulty in giving my tanks and combat cars (ACAVs with energy weapons) the fusion powerplants without which they'd be useless.

Armament required the same sort of decision. Energy weapons have major advantages over projectile weapons; but although tanks may some day mount effective lasers, I don't think an infantryman will ever be able to carry one. I therefore postulated guns that fired bolts of plasma liberated—somehow—from individual cartridges.

That took care of the hardware. The organization was basically that of the Eleventh Cav, with a few changes for the hell of it.

The unit itself was *not* based on any US unit with which I'm familiar. Its model was the French Foreign Legion; more precisely, the French Foreign Legion serving in Viet Nam just after World War Two—when most of its personnel were veterans of the SS who'd fled from Germany ahead of the Allied War Crimes Commission.

The incident around which I plotted THE BUTCHER'S BILL was the capture of Snuol the day before I arrived in Cambodia. That was the only significant fighting during the invasion of Cam-

bodia, just as Snuol was the only significant town
our forces reached.

G, one of the line troops, entered Snuol first.
There was a real street, lined with stucco-faced
shops instead of the grass huts on posts in the
farming hamlets of the region. The C-100 Anti-
Aircraft Company, a Viet Cong unit, was defending the town with a quartet of fifty-one caliber
machineguns.

A fifty-one cal could put its rounds through an
ACAV the long way, and the aluminum hull of a
Sheridan wasn't much more protection. Before G
Troop could get out, the concealed guns had de-
stroyed one of either type of vehicle.

The squadron commander responded by sending in H Company, his tanks.

The eleven M48s rolled down the street in line
ahead. The first tank slanted its main gun to the
right side of the street, the second to the left, and
so on. Each tank fired a round of canister or
shrapnel into every structure that slid past the
muzzle of its 90 mm gun.

On the other side of Snuol, they formed up
to go back again. There wasn't any need to do
that.

The VC had opened fire at first. The crews of
the M48s didn't know that, because the noise
inside was so loud that the clang of two-ounce
bullets hitting the armor was inaudible. Some of
the slugs flattened and were there on the fenders
to be picked up afterwards. The surviving VC
fled, leaving their guns behind.

There was a little looting—a bottle of whiskey, a
sack of ladies' slippers, a step-through Honda (which
was flown back to Quan Loi in a squadron helicop-

ter). But for all practical purposes, Snuol ceased to
have human significance the moment H Company
blasted its way down the street.

The civilian population? It had fled before the
shooting started.

Not that it would have made any difference to
the operation.

So I wrote a story about what wars cost and
how decisions get made in the field—despite
policy considerations back in air-conditioned
offices. It was the best story I'd written so far,
and the first time I'd tackled issues of real importance.

Only problem was, THE BUTCHER'S BILL
didn't sell.

Mostly it just got rejection slips, but one very
competent editor said that Joe Haldeman and Jerry
Pournelle were writing as much of that sort of
story as his magazine needed. (Looking back, I
find it interesting that in 1973 magazine terms,
the stories in THE FOREVER WAR, THE MER-
CENARY, and HAMMER'S SLAMMERS were
indistinguishable.)

One editor felt that THE BUTCHER'S BILL
demanded too much background, both SF and
military, for the entry-level anthology he was planning. That was a good criticism, to which I responded by writing UNDER THE HAMMER.

UNDER THE HAMMER had a new recruit as
its viewpoint character, a kid who was terrified
that he was going to make an ignorant mistake and
get himself killed. (I didn't have to go far to find a
model for the character. Remember that I hadn't
had advanced combat training before I became an
ad hoc tank crewman.) Because the recruit knew

so little, other characters could explain details to him and to the reader.

I made the kid a recruit to Hammer's Slammers, because I already had that background clear in my mind. I hadn't intended to write a series, it just happened that way.

UNDER THE HAMMER didn't sell either.

I went about a year and a half with no sales. This was depressing, and I was as prone as the next guy to whine "My stuff's better 'n some of the crap they publish."

In hindsight, I've decided that when an author doesn't sell, it's because:

1) he's doing something wrong; or

2) he's doing something different, and he isn't good enough to get away with being different.

In my case, there was some of both. The two Hammer stories were different—and clumsy; I was new to the job. Most of the other fiction I wrote during that period just wasn't very good.

But the situation was very frustrating.

The dam broke when Gordy Dickson took THE BUTCHER'S BILL for an anthology he was editing. It wasn't a lot of money, but I earned my living as an attorney. This was a sale, and it had been a long time coming.

Almost immediately thereafter, the editor at GALAXY (who'd rejected the Hammer stories) was replaced by his assistant, a guy named Jim Baen. Jim took the pair and asked for more.

I wrote three more stories in the series before Jim left to become SF editor of Ace Books. One of the three was the only piece I've written about

Colonel Hammer himself instead of Hammer's Slammers. It was to an editorial suggestion: tell how it all started. Jim took that one, and though he rejected the other two, they sold elsewhere. The dam really had broken.

I moved away from Hammer and into other things, including a fantasy novel. Then Jim, now at Ace, asked for a collection of the 35,000 words already written plus enough new material in the series to fill out a book. Earlier I'd had an idea that seemed too complex to be done at a length a magazine would buy from me. I did it—HANG-MAN—for the collection and added a little end-cap for the volume also—STANDING DOWN.

To stand between the stories, I wrote essays explaining the background of the series, social and economic as well as the hardware. In some cases I had to work out the background for the first time. I hadn't started with the intention of writing a series.

HAMMER'S SLAMMERS came out in 1979. That was the end of the series, so far as I was concerned. But as the years passed, I did a novelet. Then the setting turned out to be perfect for my effort at using the plot of the ODYSSEY as an SF novel (CROSS THE STARS). I did a short novel, AT ANY PRICE, that was published with the earlier novelet and a story I did for the volume. . . .

And I'm going to do more stories besides this one in the series, because Hammer's Slammers have become a vehicle for a message that I think needs to be more widely known. Veterans who've written or talked to me already understand, but a lot of other people don't.

When you send a man out with a gun, you

create a policymaker. When his ass is on the line, he will do whatever he needs to do.

And if the implications of that bother you, the time to do something about it is before you decide to send him out.

Dave Drake
Chapel Hill, N.C.

Here is an excerpt from Vernor Vinge's new novel, Marooned in Realtime, *coming in June 1987 from Baen Books:*

The town nestled in the foothills of the Indonesian Alps, high enough so that equatorial heat and humidity was moderated to an almost uniform pleasantness. Here the Korolevs and their friends had finally assembled the rescued from all the ages. At the moment the population was less than two hundred, every living human being. They needed more; Yelén Korolev knew where to get one hundred more. She was determined to rescue them.

Steven Fraley, President of the Republic of New Mexico, was determined that those hundred remain unrescued. He was still arguing the case when Wil Brierson arrived. ". . . and you don't appreciate the history of our era, madam. The Peacers came near to exterminating the human race. Sure, saving this group will get you a few more warm bodies, but you risk the survival of our whole colony, of the entire human race, in doing so."

Yelén Korolev looked calm, but Wil knew her well enough to recognize the signs of an impending explosion: there were rosy patches on her cheeks, yet her features were otherwise even paler than usual. She ran a hand through her blond hair. "Mr. Fraley, I really do know the history of your era. Remember that almost all of us—no matter what our present age and experience— have our childhoods within a couple hundred years of one another. The Peace Authority"—her lips twitched in a quick smile at the name—"may have started the general war of 1997. They may even be responsible for the terrible plagues of the early twenty-first century. But as governments go, they were relatively benign. This group in Kampuchea"—she waved toward the north— "went into stasis in 2048, when the Peacers were overthrown. That was before decent health care was available. It's entirely possible that none of the original criminals are present."

Fraley opened and closed his mouth, but no words

came. Finally: "Haven't you heard of their 'Renaissance' scheme? In '48 they were ready to kill by the millions again. Those guys under Kampuchea probably got more hell-bombs than a dog has fleas. That base was their secret ace in the hole. If they hadn't screwed up their stasis, they'd've come out in 2100 and blown us away. And you probably wouldn't even have been born—"

Yelén cut into the torrent. "Hell-bombs? Popguns. Even you know that. Mr. Fraley, getting another hundred people into our colony will make our settlement just big enough to survive. Marta and I haven't spent our lives setting this up just to see it die like the undermanned attempts of the past. The only reason we postponed the founding of Korolev till megayear fifty was so we could rescue those Peacers when their bobble bursts."

She turned to her partner. "Is everybody accounted for?"

Marta Korolev had sat through the argument in silence, her dark features relaxed, her eyes closed. Her headband put her in communication with the estate's autonomous devices. No doubt she had managed a half dozen fliers during the last half hour, scouring the countryside for any truant colonists the Korolev satellites had spotted. Now she opened her eyes. "Everybody's accounted for and safe. In fact"—she caught sight of Wil standing at the back of the amphitheater and grinned—"almost everyone is here on the castle grounds. I think we can provide you people with quite a show this afternoon." She either hadn't followed or—more likely—had chosen to ignore the dispute between Yelén and Fraley.

"Okay, let's get started." A rustle of anticipation passed through the audience. Many were from the twenty-first century, like Wil. But they'd seen enough of the advanced travelers to know that such a statement was more than enough signal for spectacular events to happen.

From his place at the top of the amphitheater, Wil

had a good view to the north. The forests of the higher elevations fell away to a gray-green blur that was the equatorial jungle. Beyond that, haze obscured even the existence of the Inland Sea. Even on the rare, clear day when the sea mists lifted, the Kampuchean Alps were hidden beyond the horizon. Nevertheless, the rescue should be visible; he was a bit surprised that the bluish white of the northern horizon was undisturbed.

"Things will get more exciting, I promise." Yelén's voice brought his eyes back to the stage. Two large displays floated behind her.

"As Mr. Fraley says, the Peacer bobble was supposed to be a secret. It was originally underground. It is much further underground now—somebody blundered. What was to be a fifty-year jump became something . . . longer. As near as we can figure, their bobble should burst sometime in the next few thousand years; they've been in stasis fifty million years. During that time, continents drifted and new rifts formed. Parts of Kampuchea slid deep beneath new mountains." The display behind her lit with a multicolored transect of the Kampuchean Alps. The surface crust appeared as blue, shading into yellow and orange at the greater depths. Right at the margin of orange and magma red was a tiny black disk—the Peacer bobble, afloat against the ceiling of hell.

Inside the bobble, time was stopped. Those within were as they'd been at that instant of a near-forgotten war when the losers decided to escape to the future. No force could affect a bobble's contents; no force could affect its duration—not the heart of a star, not the heart of a lover.

But when the bobble burst, when the stasis ended . . . The Peacers were about forty kilometers down. There would be a moment of noise and heat and pain as the magma swallowed them. One hundred men and women would die, and a certain endangered species would move one more step toward final extinction.

The Korolevs proposed to raise the bobble to the

surface, where it would be safe for the few remaining millennia of its duration. Yelén waved at the display. "This was taken just before we started the operation. Here's the ongoing view."

The picture flickered. The red magma boundary had risen thousands of meters above the bobble. Pinheads of white light flashed in the orange and yellow that represented the solid crust. In the place of each of those lights, red blossomed and spread, almost—Wil winced at the thought—like blood from a stab wound. "Each of those sparkles is a hundred-megaton bomb. In the last few seconds, we've released more energy than all mankind's wars put together."

The red spread as the wounds coalesced into a vast hemorrhage in the bosom of Kampuchea. The magma was still twenty kilometers below ground level. The bombs were timed so there was a constant sparkling just above the highest level of red, bringing the melt closer and closer to the surface. At the bottom of the display, the Peacer bobble floated, serene and untouched. On this scale, its motion towards the surface was imperceptible.

Wil pulled his attention from the display and looked beyond the amphitheater. There was no change: the northern horizon was still haze and pale blue. The rescue site was fifteen hundred kilometers away, but even so, he'd expected something spectacular.

The elapsed-time clock on the display showed almost four minutes. The Korolev pattern of bomb bursts was still thousands of meters short of the surface.

President Fraley rose from his seat. "Madame Korolev, please. There is still time to stop this. I know you've rescued all types, cranks, joyriders, criminals, victims. But these are *monsters*." For once, Wil thought he heard sincerity—perhaps even fear—in the New Mexican's voice. *And he might be right.* If the rumors were true, if the Peacers had created the plagues of the early twenty-first century, then they were responsible for the deaths of billions. If they had succeeded with their Renaissance Project, they would have killed most of the survivors.

Yelén Korolev glanced down at Fraley but didn't reply. The New Mexican stiffened, then waved abruptly to his people. One hundred men and women—most in NM fatigues—came quickly to their feet. It was a dramatic gesture, if nothing else: the amphitheater would be almost empty with them gone.

"Mr. President, I suggest you and the others sit back down." It was Marta Korolev. Her tone was as pleasant as ever, but the insult in the words brought a flush to Steve Fraley's face. He gestured angrily and turned to the stone steps that led from the theater.

The ground shock arrived an instant later.

320 pp. • 65647-3 • $3.50

To order any Baen Book by mail, send the cover price plus 75 cents for first-class postage and handling to: Baen Books, Dept. B, 260 Fifth Avenue, New York, N.Y. 10001.

Here is an excerpt from the new novel by Timothy Zahn, coming from Baen Books in August 1987:

TIMOTHY ZAHN
TRIPLET

The way house had been quiet for over an hour by the time Karyx's moon rose that night, its fingernail-clipping crescent adding only token assistance to the dim starlight already illuminating the grounds. Sitting on the mansion's garret-floor widow's walk, his back against the door, Ravagin watched the moon drift above the trees to the east and listened to the silence of the night. And tried to decide what in blazes he was going to do.

There actually *were* precedents for this kind of situation: loose precedents, to be sure, and hushed up like crazy by the people upstairs in the Crosspoint Building, but precedents nonetheless. Every so often a Courier and his group would have such a mutual falling out that continuing on together was out of the question . . . and when that happened the Courier would often simply give notice and quit, leaving the responsibility for getting the party back to Threshold in the hands of the nearest way house staff. Triplet management ground their collective teeth when it happened, but they'd long ago come to the reluctant conclusion that clients were better off alone than with a Courier who no longer gave a damn about their safety.

And Ravagin wouldn't even have to endure the

usual froth-mouthed lecture that would be waiting when he got back. He was finished with the Corps, and those who'd bent his fingers into taking this trip had only themselves to blame for the results. He could leave a note with Melentha, grab a horse, and be at the Cairn Mounds well before daylight. By the time Danae had finished sputtering, he'd have alerted the way house master in Feymar Protectorate on Shamsheer and be on a sky-plane over the Ordarl Mountains . . . and by the time she made it back through to Threshold and screamed for vengeance, he'd have picked up his last paychit, said bye-and-luck to Corah, and boarded a starship for points unknown. Ravagin, the great veteran Courier, actually deserting a client. Genuinely one for the record books.

Yes. He would do it. He would. Right now. He'd get up, go downstairs, and get the hell out of here.

Standing up, he gazed out at the moon . . . and slammed his fist in impotent fury on the low railing in front of him.

He couldn't do it.

"Damn," he muttered under his breath, clenching his jaw hard enough to hurt. "Damn, damn, *damn*."

He hit the railing again and inhaled deeply, exhaling in a hissing sigh of anger and resignation. He couldn't do it. No matter what the justification—no matter that the punishment would be light or nonexistent—no matter even that others had done it without lasting stigma. He was a *professional*, damn it, and it was his job to stay with his clients no matter what happened.

Danae had wounded his pride. Deserting her, unfortunately, would hurt it far more deeply then she ever could.

In other words, a classic no-win situation. With him on the short end.

And it left him just two alternatives: continue his silent treatment toward Danae for the rest of the trip, or work through his anger enough to at least get back on civil terms with her. At the moment, neither choice was especially attractive.

Out in the grounds, a flicker of green caught his eye. He looked down, frowning, trying to locate the source. Nothing was moving; nothing seemed out of place. Could there be something skulking in the clumps of trees, or perhaps even the shadows thrown by the bushes?

Or could something have tried to break through the post line?

Nothing was visible near the section of post line he could see. Cautiously, he began easing his way around the widow's walk, muttering a spirit-protection spell just to be on the safe side.

Still nothing. He'd reached the front of the house and was starting to continue past when a movement through the gap in the tree hedge across the grounds to the south caught his attention. He peered toward it . . . and a few seconds later it was repeated further east.

A horseman on the road toward Besak, most likely . . . except that Besak had long since been sealed up for the night by the village lar. And Karyx was not a place to casually indulge in nighttime travel. Whoever it was, he was either on an errand of dire emergency or else—

Or else hurrying away from an aborted attempt to break in?

Ravagin pursed his lips. "*Haklarast*," he said. It was at least worth checking out.

The glow-fire of the sprite appeared before him. "I am here, as you summoned," it squeaked.

"There's a horse and human traveling on the road toward Besak just south of here," he told it. "Go to the human and ask why he rides so late. Return to me with his answer."

The sprite flared and was gone. Ravagin watched it dart off across the darkened landscape and then, for lack of anything better to do while he waited, continued his long-range inspection of the post line. Again he found nothing; and he was coming around to the front of the house again when the sprite returned. "What answer?" he asked it.

"None. The human is not awake."

"Are you sure?" Ravagin asked, frowning. He'd once learned the hard way about the hazards of sleeping on horseback—most Karyx natives weren't stupid enough to try it. "Really asleep, not injured?"

"I do not know."

Of course it wouldn't—spirits didn't see the world the way humans did. "Well . . . is he riding alone, or is there a spirit with him protecting him from falls?"

"There is a djinn present, though it is not keeping the human from falling. There is no danger of that."

And with a djinn along to— "What do you mean? Why isn't he going to fall?"

"The human is upright, in full control of the animal—"

"Wait a second," Ravagin cut it off. "You just told me he was asleep. How can he be controlling the horse?"

"The human is asleep," the sprite repeated, and Ravagin thought he could detect a touch of vexation in the squeaky voice. "It is in control of its animal."

"That's impossible," Ravagin growled. "He'd have to be—"

Sleepwalking.

"Damn!" he snarled, eyes darting toward the place where the rider had vanished, thoughts skidding with shock, chagrin, and a full-bellied rush of fear. *Danae*—

His mental wheels caught. "Follow the rider," he ordered the sprite. "Stay back where you won't be spotted by any other humans, but don't let her out of your sight. First give me your name, so I can locate you later. Come on, give—I haven't got time for games."

"I am Psskapsst," the sprite said reluctantly.

"Psskapsst, right. Now get after it—and *don't* communicate with that djinn."

The glow-fire flared and skittered off. Racing along the widow's walk, Ravagin reached the door and hurried inside. Danae's room was two flights down, on the second floor; on a hunch, he stopped first on the third floor and let himself into Melentha's sanctum.

The place had made Ravagin's skin crawl even with good lighting, and the dark shadows stretching around the room now didn't improve it a bit. Shivering reflexively, he stepped carefully around the central pentagram and over to the table where Melentha had put the bow and Coven robe when she'd finished her spirit search.

The robe was gone.

Swearing under his breath, he turned and hurried back to the door—and nearly ran into Melentha as she suddenly appeared outside in the hallway. "What are you doing in there?" she demanded, holding her robe closed with one hand and clutching a glowing dagger in the other.

"The Coven robe's gone," he told her, "and I think Danae's gone with it."

"What?" She backed up hastily to let him pass, then hurried to catch up with him. "When?"

"Just a little while ago—I think I saw her leaving on horseback from the roof. I just want to make sure—"

They reached Danae's room and Ravagin pushed open the door . . . and she was indeed gone.

August 1987 • 384 pp. • 65341-5 • $3.50

Here is an excerpt from IRON MASTER by Patrick Tilley, to be published in July 1987 by Baen Books. It is the third book in the "Amtrak Series," which also includes CLOUD WARRIOR and THE FIRST FAMILY.

PATRICK TILLEY
IRON MASTER

The five sleek craft, under the control of their newly-trained samurai pilots, lifted off the grass and thundered skywards, trailing thin blue ribbons of smoke from their solid-fuel rocket tubes. Levelling off at a thousand feet, they circled the field in a tight arrowhead formation, then dived and pulled up into a loop, rolling upright as they came down off the top to go into a second—the maneuver once known as the Immelmann turn.

There was a gasp from the crowd as the lines of blue smoke were suddenly severed from the diving aircraft. A tense, eerie silence descended. The first rocket boosters had reached the end of their brief lives. Time for the second burn. The machines continued their downward plunge—then, with a reassuring explosion of sound, a stabbing white-hot finger of flame appeared beneath the cockpit pod of the lead aircraft. Two, three, four—five!

The watching crowd of Iron Masters responded with a deep-throated roar of approval. Cadillac, who was positioned in front of the stand immediately below his patrons, Yama-Shita and Min-Ota, swelled with pride. These were the kind of people he could identify with. Harsh, forbidding, and cruel, with unbelieveably rigid social mores, they nevertheless appreciated and placed great value on beautiful objects, whether they be works of nature or some article fashioned by their craft-masters. Cadillac knew his flying machines appealed to the Iron Masters' aesthetic sensibilities. Like the proud horses of the domain lords, they were lithe and graceful, and the echoing thunder that marked their passage through the sky conveyed the same feeling of irresistible power as the hoofbeats of their galloping steeds. Here, in the Land of the Rising Sun, he had been taken seriously, had been given the opportunity to demonstrate his true capabilities, and had been accorded the praise and esteem Mr. Snow had always denied him. And his work here was only just beginning!

As the five aircraft nosed over the top of the second loop, leaving a blue curve of smoke behind them, their booster rockets exploded in rapid succession. Boooomm! Ba-ba-boom-boomm. Booom!

Cadillac, along with everyone else in the stand behind him, watched in speechless horror as each one was engulfed by a ball of flame. The slender silk-covered spruce wings were ripped to pieces and consumed. On the ground below, confusion reigned as the shower of burning debris spiralled down towards the packed review stand, preceded by the rag-doll bodies of the pilots.

Steve Brickman, gliding high above the lake some three miles to the south of the Heron Pool, saw the fireballs blossom and fall. It had worked. The rocket burn had ignited the explosive charge he, Jodi, and Kelso had packed with loving care into the second of the three canisters each aircraft carried beneath its belly. Now there could be no turning back. Steve caught himself invoking the name of Mo-Town—praying that everything would go according to plan.

General To-Shiba, seated on his left, was quite unaware of the disaster. Fascinated by the bird's-eye view of his large estate, the military governor's eyes were fixed on the small island in the middle of the lake two thousand feet below. It was here, in the summer house surrounded by trees and a beautiful rock garden, that Clearwater was held prisoner. The beautiful creature who was now his body-slave and who possessed that rarest of gifts—lustrous, sweet-smelling body hair. The thought of his next visit filled him with pleasurable anticipation. As a samurai, To-Shiba had no fear of death but, at that moment, he had no inkling his demise was now only minutes away. . . .

July 1987 • 416 pp. • 65338-5 • $3.95

To order any Baen Book, send the cover price plus 75¢ for first-class postage and handling to: Baen Books, Dept. BB, 260 Fifth Avenue, New York, N.Y. 10001.

ROBERT A. HEINLEIN

"Heinlein knows more about blending provocative scientific thinking with strong human stories than any dozen other contemporary science fiction writers."
—*Chicago Sun-Times*

"Robert A. Heinlein wears imagination as though it were his private suit of clothes. What makes his work so rich is that he combines his lively, creative sense with an approach that is at once literate, informed, and exciting."
—*New York Times*

Seven of Robert A. Heinlein's best-loved titles are now available in superbly packaged new Baen editions, with embossed series-look covers by artist John Melo. Collect them all by sending in the order form below:

TRAVIS SHELTON
LIKES BAEN BOOKS
BECAUSE THEY TASTE GOOD

Recently we received this letter from Travis Shelton of Dayton, Texas:

I have come to associate Baen Books with Del Monte. Now what is that supposed to mean? Well, if you're in a strange store with a lot of different labels, you pick Del Monte because the product will be consistent and will not disappoint.

Something I have noticed about Baen Books is that the stories are always fast-paced, exciting, action-filled and seem to be published because of content instead of who wrote the book. I now find myself glancing to see who published the book instead of reading the back or intro. If it's a Baen Book it's going to be good and exciting and will capture your spare reading moments.

Another discovery I have recently made is that I don't have any Baen Books in my unread stacks—and I read four to seven books a week, so that in itself is a meaningful statistic.

Why do you like Baen Books? Drop us a letter like Travis did. The person who best tells us what we're doing right—and where we could do better—will receive a Baen Books gift certificate worth $100. Entries must be received by December 31, 1987. Send to Baen Books, 260 Fifth Avenue, New York, N.Y. 10001. And ask for our free catalog!